PRAISE FOR MARIE DARRI

'There are few writers who may have changed my perception of the world, but Darrieussecq is one of them.' *The Times*

'The internationally celebrated author who illuminates those parts of life other writers cannot or do not want to reach.' *Independent*

'Shatters taboos, simplifications and affectations.'
Magazine Littéraire

'I absolutely adored this account of sexual awakening.' *L'Express*

'This clever novel, *Clèves* [*All the Way*], is both personal and universal—and without the slight trace of sentimentality.' *Libération*

'*Tom Is Dead* is powerful; when one has finished reading it one feels it absolutely needed to exist.' NANCY HUSTON

'*Tom Is Dead* is mesmerising and deeply rewarding....impressive in its evocation of vastly different worlds and lives.'
Australian Literary Review

'Darrieussecq is as daring as she is original...
a singular new voice.' *Irish Times*

'She makes all those daring young men of letters look very tame indeed.' *Herald* (Glasgow)

'Her gifts are dazzling.' *Observer*

'I love the way Marie Darrieussecq writes about the world as if it were an extension of herself and her feelings.'
J.M.G LE CLÉZIO, Nobel Laureate for Literature 2008

'Another astonishing work by Darrieussecq. *All the Way* is a stunning achievement.' M.J. HYLAND

MARIE DARRIEUSSECQ was born in 1969 in Bayonne, France. Her debut novel, *Pig Tales*, was published in thirty-four countries. Four other novels have also been translated into English, *My Phantom Husband*, *A Brief Stay With the Living*, *White* and *Tom Is Dead*. Marie Darrieussecq lives in Paris with her husband and children.

PENNY HUESTON is a senior editor at Text Publishing.

ALL THE WAY

Marie Darrieussecq

Translated by Penny Hueston

TEXT PUBLISHING MELBOURNE AUSTRALIA

textpublishing.com.au

The Text Publishing Company
Swann House
22 William Street
Melbourne Victoria 3000
Australia

First published in French as *Clèves* by P.O.L editeur, 2011
First published in English by The Text Publishing Company, 2013

Design by WH Chong
Typeset by J&M Typesetting

Printed in Australia by Griffin Press, an Accredited ISO AS/NZS 14001:2004 Environmental Management System printer.

National Library of Australia Cataloguing-in-Publication entry : (pbk)
Author: Darrieussecq, Marie.
Title: All the way / by Marie Darrieussecq ; translated by Penny Hueston.
ISBN: 9781921922732 (pbk.)
ISBN: 9781921921537 (ebook)
Subjects: Teenage girls—Fiction.
Other Authors/Contributors: Hueston, Penny.
Dewey Number: 843.914

This book is printed on paper certified against the Forest Stewardship Council® Standards. Griffin Press holds FSC chain-of-custody certification SGS-COC-005088. FSC promotes environmentally responsible, socially beneficial and economically viable management of the world's forests.

‘Is it possible that we know nothing about girls, who exist nonetheless? Is it possible that we say “women”, “children”, “boys”, and don’t imagine—in spite of all our education, we don’t imagine that it’s been a long time since these words…’

Rainer Maria Rilke,
The Notebooks of Malte Laurids Brigge

CONTENTS

I

GETTING IT

'Go on then, off you go to your carnival.'

Ten in the evening, June. Her parents have guests. They are drinking rosé. 'Go on then, off you go to your carnival.' Their friends whistle when she appears in her dress. Her mother kisses her and then rubs her cheek to remove the lipstick. Her father gives her a ten-franc note.

Solange skips along the road, a little hop with each step, a skidding noise, *tchiff, tchiff*. Her dress flaps against the backs of her knees. There are red dogs embroidered along the edge of the hem. It's her favourite dress.

She passes Monsieur Bihotz's house; she's glad he's not out the front.

The crowd surges and she hears 'your father, your father'. She looks up at the church tower. The hands on the clock make an angle like an index finger and thumb, a pistol. A quarter to twelve. She was allowed out until eleven-thirty.

Shit shit. Nathalie's gaping mouth: a moist, red 'your father'.

She can see him. Completely naked. A red scarf around his neck, his Air Inter cap on his head. With his mate Georges who is also naked. They're singing a song about a priest and a nun. 'You're going to bless our dicks!' shouts her father as he runs towards her. No, towards the priest behind her. Her father's dick, a wobbling white willy, is very different from Monsieur Bihotz's.

As if it wasn't difficult enough at school already. Especially as she's the only one who doesn't go to Sunday school. Raphaël Bidegarraï from Grade Six, his hands cupped over his fly, asks her to bless his dick.

Nathalie's mother has lent her a prayer book and she's practising in her room. *Baby Jesus, may you protect my parents and bring peace to their spirits. And forgive us our trespasses as we forgive those who trespass against us.* She asks her mother: *What does trespass mean?* 'It's when you can't express who you really are. For example, when I do housework while his job is to fly a plane.'

And deliver us from temptation. She recites twenty Our Fathers every night. She turns the bedspread down in folds of precisely equal width. Neither her feet nor her hands must touch the edges of the mattress, and her head must be exactly in the centre of the pillow.

Behind the church there is a statue of the Virgin Mary

in a blue and white dress shaped like a tube, from which her hands, her head and her halo emerge.

Hail Mary, full of grace, our Lord is with thee. Blessed art thou among women, and blessed is the fruit of thy womb, Jesus. Holy Mary, mother of God, pray for us sinners, now and in the hour of our death. Amen.

Ten times. Hands, feet, head exactly in the centre of the pillow. When she sleeps over at Monsieur Bihotz's, he chucks everything on the floor when he comes to tuck her in.

Monsieur Bihotz says that her father just wanted to have fun and that's a good thing in a person.

All children are like the children in that film, *Village of the Damned*, where aliens come one night and inseminate women who can't remember anything about it afterwards. She saw it on television. The pale-coloured eyes of a pale child. The shock lasted only a second, that instant when she saw herself. Those eyes looking at her, that ashen stranger with the too-bright eyes who is her, pale as death, who forces her to truss up her bed in a thousand ways, and to cover any bit of her that is hanging out. Except when she slides in next to Monsieur Bihotz and his huge body protects her.

Nathalie says that you can tell the priest everything, and that actually you should, so you're forgiven for your bad thoughts and your bad actions. But her father's dick?

She'd like to know if she's good or bad inside. Exactly

what there is inside her. Perhaps she'll swallow a spider. It'll wriggle and wiggle and tiggle inside her. She doesn't know why. Perhaps she'll die!

The whole school is obsessed by sex. Raphaël Bidegarraï asks her if she knows what a whore is. He explains it to her, patiently, in a state of aroused pity.

She's not quite sure about kissing. 'We can kiss those bastards goodbye,' says her father. 'Give me a kiss,' says Monsieur Bihotz. 'I wonder what she looks like when she comes,' says Georges, talking about an air hostess. She understands that those particular words have a direct connection to 'whore'. She understands the word; she'll always understand it, her whole life long. A before and an after in the understanding of the word whore. Inside a little girl, there is a whore.

Raphaël Bidegarraï, who's always been the biggest of them all, makes the girls stand in a row with the boys facing them. The girls lift up their skirts and the boys touch their panties.

Peggy Salami already has a tricky name. The day he gets her naked, everyone sees (she's glad it's not her) the slit between her legs, marked out by a dividing compass, two halves of a sphere, from the base of the belly to the base of the back, two sections perfectly joined but slightly parted, neatly bifurcating the body, as well as the class, the village and the world, and anatomically much more rational than what her father and Monsieur Bihotz and presumably all men have.

Her mother's body is the same. Pubic hair hides the front part, but her buttocks are there at the back. In summer she spends Sundays naked on the terrace, lying on one side then the other so she can tan without getting lines, and complaining that the sea is so far away. It's a lot harder to imagine what happened at Madame Bihotz's house. Madame Bihotz: a pyramid shape under a nylon smock. So fat that the slit, if there was a slit, must have closed up.

In the evening Monsieur Bihotz used to undress his mother and put her to bed. Beneath her smock she wore a giant petticoat. Under her arms it was like she had extra breasts. Solange used to climb up into the high bed where, bearded and scrubbed clean, Madame Bihotz would read her *Tom Thumb*, or *Little Red Riding Hood*, in the old versions that are really scary.

On Sunday mornings Monsieur Bihotz would take his mother to church in a wheelchair. He pushed her from their house into town. It took them half an hour because it was so steep. On the way back it was much quicker; he only had to be a counterweight. From the terrace, her father used to call them to watch the performance, *mère et fils* Bihotz battling the bulk.

*

On Sunday mornings her father sometimes took her driving. He let her sit in the front seat of his Alpine sports car. They had fun sputtering up the hills and hurtling straight down beneath the silos, *vroooom, vroom.* Then they drove back towards the river and the edge of town, and stopped to buy cakes. From there they had two choices: the sea, an hour away, or the marina, five minutes away.

They parked in front of the marina and ate their cakes. Her father told her stories about his emergency landings, about cumulonimbus suction drafts and about the time when the idiot air hostess had forgotten to release the escape chutes. He told her: 'At Clèves we don't have the sea but we have a pretty lake.'

He had a smoke with Georges at the Yacht Club. On the wall there was a calendar with naked pin-up girls. Every so often they parked in a vacant lot at the housing development. Her father would leave her with the cakes and the radio on and come back later.

She looked out at the still water. Gusts of wind shook the car. She opened the window a bit. The wind whipped steely grey scribble marks over the surface of the water. It brushed her cheeks. She moved across behind the steering wheel. She changed gears standing up on the pedals, then sat down again. The road stretched out ahead, crisscrossed with deer, lined with staring hares. Or she was on board a plane and she was flipping the little switches in the roof. The motors were roaring, she tilted the steering wheel and gained speed, the ground slipped away, she took off in a flash and the lake became smaller, a scrap of blue.

It's amazing how everything changes, from one house to the next. What must it be like, for example, to go from a Mongolian yurt to an American skyscraper, if there's already such a huge difference between her parents' house and Monsieur Bihotz's house (or Rose's)?

Her mother brought her a stool from her shop; it was in the shape of a Coca-Cola can. And curtains with a Statue of Liberty print for her birthday. And Monsieur Bihotz gave her a poster that she loves, the word *WHY?* written above a dead soldier, but her mother says it's not appropriate for someone her age.

Rose's bedroom is completely different. It feels light, delicate. Even the walls are different, the shape of the bedroom is different. You'd need a completely new word, especially when you think about Monsieur Bihotz's bedroom, with the poster of France Gall and the stacks of *Sud-Ouest* newspapers and the filthy coffee cups.

Her father says that Rose's house smells like roses. The Bihotz house smells like dog and soup, or rather it used to smell like soup, when Madame Bihotz was there making it. Madame Bihotz's bedroom smells like something inert. Perhaps dust. Close up, the dust looks like bits of fluffy wool, or ash. At the shop her mother is always dusting, because of the passing traffic. Her mother claims the dust is getting worse.

Her parents' room is brown. The curtains are orange and floral. Two matching lamps sit on two velvet bedside tables. When her mother is home, she's always in bed. On her mother's side of the bed is a photograph of a little boy.

She puts her hand in front of her eyes and tries removing one of the items, the bed, a lamp, the photo, and the whole thing is transformed, it's no longer the same room, one tiny thing changes everything. And when her father is there, everything is different again.

She is lying on one of the school desks, the ones with a hole for the inkwell. Raphaël Bidegarraï, Christian Goyenetche, Nathalie, Rose, Delphine Peyreborde, the two Villebarrouin kids, all the Boursenave kids, even the little Lavinasse kids, everyone is there. Superimposed heads, pairs of eyes like pinheads, and each kid sticks a pin into her body. Red pins like the ones the teacher uses to fix the map to the wall—carefully, one by one, taking it in turns. The pressure beneath her hand increases, the hard, hot spot that is the point of it all, from pinprick to pinprick, the whole class, everyone around her. She's not tied down but it's impossible to move, just as impossible for her to get away as it is for a naughty student to escape the corner of the classroom.

She submits and the pins stick into her one by one, slow, deep, her hand rubbing the vital spot, her legs spread wide apart, the unbearable pleasure has to last longer, and when the teacher sticks in the final pin, the indescribable instant of climax—she can fall asleep, in her childhood bed, the sheets scarcely rumpled.

She used to open the big bottle of *Bien Être* eau de Cologne and Madame Bihotz would spring out, flamboyant, like a genie, along with her whole bedroom and her nylon blouses. Then, even though she took deep breaths, Madame Bihotz would disappear into the static memory of a fat, seated woman. She had to put the lid back on the bottle and force herself to forget. And then start again, and Madame Bihotz would spring out again.

'You can have her bedroom,' Monsieur Bihotz told her. Snuffling and hugging her tight. Hot and moist like a giant mouth.

On top of Madame Bihotz's bed there were three soft-toy dogs. And the real live dog in the middle, called Lulu, a bitch. Lulu was looking more and more like Madame Bihotz.

Are dead people still nice when they're dead?

She preferred Monsieur Bihotz's bedroom, with its posters of motorbikes and France Gall.

At 11.30 p.m. exactly, her father's plane flew over the rooftops. She snuggled up to Monsieur Bihotz. 'It's Papa's plane,' she whispered, sucking her thumb, and he told her to stop, she was too old for that.

Papa's mother, whom we called Nannie, called her Nono, which has nothing to do with Solange unless you mean Soso. 'Solange,' corrected her mother. 'Yes, Nono,' repeated Nannie, and on it went. 'How you've grown, Nono. What a cute little thing you are, Nono.' Nannie was like Papa, prone to shocking fits of rage: 'Oh, come on! I'm not making things up. I know exactly what I'm talking about.' We were on our way back from her house in the Alpine sports car, complaining about how gaga Nannie was getting.

When Nannie died, Lulu started to look like her too, her chin receding (if dogs have chins), her forehead bulging more and more, the crown of her head hanging over her absence of a nose.

'My poor Monsieur Bihotz. It's hard to lose your mummy. Young as you are. But it's also a relief. You'll have to pull yourself together, keep going. Our little girl is all upset, seeing you like this.'

When Monsieur Bihotz comes into their house, and sits there on the couch, so large and upright, it's difficult to breathe: the molecules of air don't know where to line up, the walls of the house wobble. The standard lamps, the pewter trinkets, the Toffoli lithograph: it's like Monsieur Bihotz is going to turn everything upside down. You can see his sleeveless T-shirt under the shirt he has put on specially.

'Thank you for the flowers,' says her mother.

'You cut your hydrangeas,' says her father.

Monsieur Bihotz and her father in the same room, under the same roof, like animals from different species, you don't know which one eats which, herbivore or carnivore, an ox in an anthill, a dog swimming between two herons—a catastrophe waiting to happen.

She asks if she can have the bunch of hydrangeas in her bedroom. 'A real little housewife,' says her father, smiling.

('We're lucky', he'll say later, 'if it'd been Christmas, he would have given them the gold-spray treatment and we would've been landed with them for six months.' 'The worst,' her mother will add, 'are the gladioli, you know, those red things he's got under his balcony.')

Monsieur Bihotz puts a single sugar cube in his mug, whereas at his place he puts two cubes in his teacup decorated with a bird. On his hairy face you can still see the marks from when she squeezed his blackheads. Through his shirt you can glimpse his tattoos, AC/DC on one arm, and a skull and crossbones on the other. On his chest he's got a tattoo of a tiger with a rose, but that one's hidden by his T-shirt.

'He's got them on his cock,' says her father one evening,

drinking rosé with his mates. 'MY, it says, for MUMMY. I've got the same thing, GT for GET FUCKED AND GET FUCKED AGAIN TO EVERYONE WHO THINKS I'M A FUCKWIT.'

Stories of kidnapped children. Of mothers running behind cars, screaming 'my baby, my baby'. He forbids her to go out without him, even into the garden. She waits for him to wake up. Climbs on a chair and looks at the chickens, the rabbit cages, the logs of wood under a black tarpaulin. The tree with the name of an island, *albizia*. The rolls of old wire netting. The tyres. The pond at the bottom of the garden. And, at the other end, the bushes trimmed into spherical shapes, and the canna lilies. Big red flowers that look like the heads of turkeys. And the corner stubbornly covered in moss that Monsieur Bihotz weeds obsessively.

One day I'll build you a pool. You'll be able to go swimming.

From this window she can see her house. She left a naughty doll under her little desk, hanging off the trestle.

'Without you,' says Monsieur Bihotz, 'I would never get out of bed.' He makes her soldiers of buttered toast, with helmets drawn in the butter. He dips a soup spoon in a kilo-sized pot of jam. He makes her eat an apple. 'Your mother said you eat fruit.' He pushes the peeler in and flicks out the core. He screws on the lid of the electric coffee grinder. There's a terrifying noise, the coffee beans jump around and disappear in a black cloud, and Lulu barks and barks. A giant hand screws on the roof of the house and she, Bihotz and Lulu disappear, pulverised.

In the afternoon he would reheat the same pot of coffee, and say, just like Madame Bihotz used to, 'Boiled coffee is ruined coffee.' He also said, 'The late Madame Bihotz.' That's what you say for dead people.

'He's a little bit odd,' her mother used to say. 'But what would we do without him.'

Given their timetables, it seemed just as easy for her to sleep at his place, during the week anyway.

After coffee, they would go down into the basement to shuck the ears of corn. Straddling the edge of the metal tank, scraping the corn cobs between their thighs. He pounded the grains with a mallet, for the ducks. She used to go home covered in splinters and with corn husks in her hair. 'A real little farmer's wife,' her mother would say.

Madame Bihotz had been cremated. The late Madame Bihotz went up in smoke.

Madame Bihotz is in the urn. Monsieur Bihotz sleeps with it, she explained to her parents.

Her father sighed. 'Isn't there a proper nanny in the village?'

'Well, you could always look after her yourself,' her mother replied.

*

'Extroverted,' Rose says to her, 'is when you laugh, you tell stories, you dance... Your father's extroverted. Introverted is when you're a bit sad, and you look mysterious. I'm introverted. My mother is extroverted. My father is introverted. Actually my family is the opposite of your family.'

It's five o'clock, hot chocolate time; Rose's mother is in the kitchen. 'I've made a fruit loaf, girls! How are your parents? I stopped by the shop the other day. Your mother has some pretty things there at the moment.'

Rose's mother wears boots that click on the wooden floor. She sits down at the table, between the bowls of hot chocolate, wearing her short, fringed skirt. She lights a cigarette. You can see her underpants.

She's always doing disturbing things like putting a gentle hand on the back of her neck and whispering, 'So, Solange, how are you?'

Yeah, okay.

Rose's mother always wears knee-high red boots, even at home. Those boots hold her to the floor like a magnetic field.

Her father calls her a madwoman: 'She's a madwoman *and* an idiot.'

'If there was a problem, you'd tell me, wouldn't you?'

Her head tilts beneath the gentle hand. And, inexplicably, she feels water pressing at the back of her throat and behind her eyes, as if she's a jug about to spill over.

Monsieur Bihotz picked her up at six o'clock. Rose's mother insisted he stay for a drink. Rose's father came in for a minute to say hello. He always made the same joke, in a nasty voice, about her and Rose, the princesses of Clèves, and no one knew what to say. Especially Monsieur Bihotz, who looked like he was encased in a bell jar that muffled his occasional utterances, and squashed him smaller and thicker. But with Rose's mother Monsieur Bihotz behaved more or less normally. He had a Ricard and she had a whisky, and they clinked glasses.

The others started in on her as soon as she arrived at school. It was inevitable. Everything was thrown off balance, tipped over. It was vicious: suddenly all eyes were on her. It didn't happen every day, but every day it was a possibility, and there was nothing to be done about it.

A gang formed around Raphaël. The only day she cried was when they all cut a big strand of hair off the side of her head. She didn't run away. They would have made even more fun of her. She examined herself in the mirror. What was the matter with her? Was it because she didn't go to Sunday school, or was it because of her father's *extroversion*?

And yet there were so many other crazy people. The Lavinasse family had nine children, two of whom lived with their cousins the Boursenave family, who had six children themselves, none of whom could read. On the topic of crazies, Madame Bihotz died enormous but respected by everyone.

The whole school was cascading over Solange like a liquid. When Concepción González turned up at school with her ringlets, her frilly dress and not a word of French, Solange had hoped that things would change. But Concepión González slipped on a pair of jeans two days later, spoke French by the end of the month, and became best friends with everyone. She had come to the shop for a communion present. 'That little Spanish moppet is adorable. No silver spoon in *her* mouth. You'll have to be nice to her.'

Of course there was Peggy Salami, but she actually was retarded. On one of her hands she had a sixth finger without a fingernail or bones. And let's not forget the weirdest of the Boursenave sons, who clutched at his groin and rocked. Nor the Kudeshayan kids, who were called the Dogs' Arses and were darker than Africans but you must be *tolerant.*

The Boursenave kid shouted 'Faggot!' to anyone who came too close.

She was waiting for Grade Six, to leave this dump. Leave primary school behind her like a lost world of dinosaurs and fossils.

'You got scalped by the Indians?' Monsieur Bihotz asked her. And at night when he put her to bed: 'School's not that easy.' What would he know. A tiny lifebuoy in a huge flood.

*

Rose seemed different too, when she wasn't at home. That rainy day, when Raphaël put Solange's head under the drain-pipe as Roland Lavinasse and André Boursenave each pinned back one of her arms, that day of deafening rain, Rose, of course, was not holding her head under the water nor was she in the cluster of girls egging the boys on and laughing over the sound of the rain. But she had seen Rose looking across at her, standing back a bit, looking at her as if she didn't know her, or didn't recognise her. A bit upset, put out that she had got to this point, to the extreme limit of what is possible to look at, or away from. Her best friend Rose.

'I like you because you're really intelligent,' Rose had said to her over their hot chocolates. 'Even my father says so.' She was looking at her intently. 'You've got that thing not many people have. My mother has it. I've got it, too. I can't really say your mother has it; I'm not exactly sure what it is that she's lacking. Perhaps she needs to leave your father?' Rose always said the most alarming things in that incomparable syntax and elegant accent.

Was it *sexual*? Did it affect people who, like her, thought constantly about things that others didn't seem to think about?

Concepción, pretty now, a ponytail bouncing on her shoulders, was playing elastics with Rose and Nathalie. She imagined her tripping as she jumped and falling with her gob wide open onto a spoon that busted her brain. *Crack.*

*

There is also a photo in the living room. It is there just like the curtains and the pewter trinkets, and a whole pile of things that don't have a name precisely because they are just there, there from before, before her, Solange. The little boy belongs to the photo like the object hanging next to it belongs to the wall, and another object belongs to the mantelpiece. When people ask, they're told that the object on the wall is a *warming pan*; it was used in the past when there was no heating. The thing was filled up with live embers and, thanks to the long handle, the beds were *warmed*. The object on the mantelpiece is a telescope, it belonged to a great-grandfather who was a sailor.

'Go to the carnival all by yourself? At your age? All by yourself. With so many idiot drivers zooming round those bends. And *which* dress? Well, we'll see about that. The red dogs. At ten o'clock at night. Do you know what happens to girls who go to the carnival all by themselves in a dress with red dogs on it at ten o'clock at night? No, I was not sleeping. Why didn't your parents telephone me? They didn't think twice all the other times.'

Monsieur Bihotz is red, huge and swaying on his feet, but as soon as he gets too close to that topic, to her parents, he backs off. His muzzle has brushed the electric fence. He calms down.

'Come over here.' He hugs her very hard and, bending

down, rests his big head on her neck. He's got that 'mystical' look, that's Rose's word for when people get that look she finds ridiculous, like they're on another planet, unhinged from 'real life'. And he looks at the garden in silence, as if they were the only survivors on Earth. As if all that remained in the village was their house, and all that was left of humanity was the two of them.

What was worse, to go or not to go to the carnival, to risk it, hoping they all have other fish to fry, rather than stay in her room, in the shafts of the setting sun, with the blare of the brass band muffled behind the shutters, at ten o'clock at night in the month of June?

She tries to keep a diary, like Rose. Rose even gave her a Hallmark notebook for her birthday. But it's fiddly. Life is boring. Nevertheless, says Rose, we mustn't forget our youth, mustn't forget what we used to be and become old farts.

Perhaps she should tape herself. She uses the same tape recorder her father used when he tried to learn English. She presses Record:

I was allowed to go to the carnival. It was ten o'clock at night and it was hot. I put on my dress with the red dogs. I went on the dodgem cars with Rose and Christian. Rose is my best friend. Christian and I are in love. No one knows except Rose. Lots of kids from school were there but no one

She's not sure about saying 'pissed me off'.

annoyed me. I've decided to keep this diary every day from now on. Signed Solange. Top secret.

She presses Pause. The tape emits a tiny sound, as if it was groaning with the effort. She releases the Pause button.

Get stuffed anyone who listens to this.

She presses Rewind. Then Play. The tape turns with a slight *chchch*.

'It was ten o'clock at night and it was hot.' A plaintive, mannered voice. Like her mother's. Not her own voice. Rose told her that the skull is like a sound box and that the voice in your head is not the voice others hear. Oddly enough that seems to make sense to her.

In her father's car there are magazines, copies of *Jours de France* and of *Lui*. Parked in front of a house at the end of a road, as the leaves of the poplars go *poc poc* on the hood of the car, she enters into a forest of naked women. They've all got the same slit between their legs, except that it has a different effect on her than seeing Peggy Salami's slit. The women look at her straight in the eye, their fingers in their furrow, their legs spread wide. Some of them have pubic hair, some don't (like her), or almost none (like her). She grasps a few words, *panting and arched over*, a bit unusual but immediately effective. The women's gaze, and their fingers, and what else—the surprise, the need to wee from the moment she got in the car, the company of all these women, women just like her, she is just like these women, she plunges her hand inside her jeans and rubs, fast, it's a bit dry, the women are looking at her and she's *panting and arched over* and the relief is immediate, and something moist gets in her fingers, that's odd, she didn't actually wet her pants.

The Russians have invaded Afghanistan. Her mother buys kilos of sugar and flour, and bulk containers of water. 'Here we go again, just like in sixty-two,' says Georges, who's come to sample more rosé. 'The Bay of Pigs?' asks her mother. 'No, what a dimwit,' says her father, 'the Missile Crisis, but you bought sugar both times.'

She looks out at the terrace, and beyond, to Monsieur Bihotz's, his shed, the chickens and further beyond to the wooded area. In its place, she imagines an obsidian valley. She read about it in a science-fiction book. It's like black glass. Obsidian covers the whole landscape: the houses, the shed, and the crater of the dried-up pond, and the petrified tree trunks. The path up to the village is made of obsidian, and the church tower, and the people too, all in obsidian.

The missiles leave the Soviet Union and right now are heading towards the village. Georges and her father are drinking rosé and her mother is clearing up, uptight and upset as usual. Monsieur Bihotz must be watching television and all the others are tucked away in their houses too, the nine Lavinasse sons, and the six Boursenave children, and

Raphaël Bidegarraï, and Rose and her family, tucked away in Rose's house. And everything is going to vitrify. And by the time the Americans send their own missiles, they will be destroyed in turn, and the Russians will no longer exist but their missiles will still be cruising, like those vanished stars that still sparkle in the sky. And, just like the village, the entire Earth will have melted under lava that has cooled and formed into black glass. And if an extraterrestrial turns up, it will take him a while to recognise inside the glass whatever used to be alive—it will look like minuscule bees in amber, smaller than all that matter in which it is trapped.

And her mother is shouting for her to come and help her clear up, but if she stops visualising the obsidian garden it will actually happen. And they will all die, her parents, Monsieur Bihotz, Rose and Raphaël and everyone—statues of black glass.

Coupling n. The action of coupling or engaging in mating. || The coming together of two individuals of the same animal species, necessary for reproduction. (See *encycl.*) || Device used to connect two or more pieces of a machine. ENCYCL. *Coupling* has not been identified in most marine animals (sea urchins, bony fish) but it is essential to all species that reproduce outside water (insects, advanced vertebrates). It can even be found occurring among hermaphrodites (snails, earthworms).

This is in the first section of the *Nouveau Larousse universel*—just after **come** v. (*to come clean about her crimes*); (*to come the grande dame*)—and before **courage** n. (*it takes courage to stand up for your rights*). This dictionary dates from a year before she was born, as if her parents, too, needed to resort to an entry on zoological cycles in order to understand something about the distinctions between things: water/land, vegetable/animal, man/woman, dead/alive.

> **Sex** [seks] n. (lat. *sexus*, from *secare*, to cut). Each of the two complementary adult divisions of a species, the union of which guarantees reproduction. (See chart REPRODUCTION and *encycl.*) | | The organ of biological generation. | | *The weaker sex, the fair sex*, women. | | *The stronger sex*, men. ENCYCL. The difference between the sexes can be almost negligible (mushrooms, algae, sea urchins, various fish, pigeons) or enhanced by *secondary sexual characteristics* more or less accentuated (deer's antlers, cock's spur, stag beetle's mandible). Sometimes the female retains a larval characteristic (glow-worm) or, conversely, it may be the male that is the diminutive member (*ceratias* fish). A great diversity of appearance can be found among butterflies in particular. In hermaphrodite species (snails, earthworms) each individual creature is both male and female. The organ that develops the fertilising gamete (testicle in animals, stamen in plants) is called 'male'. The organ

that develops the fertilised gamete (ovary in animals, pistil in plants) is called 'female'.)

The **REPRODUCTION** chart, opposite the coloured plate of **REPTILES**, shows, in black and white, a couple of fish, a colony of aphids, algae, and an interesting-looking fleshy cap, fat and shiny, full of folds opening around a swollen knot: a **coupling** (slugs). In one corner there is a label **AUTOFERTILISATION** ('very rare: Barberry plant, tapeworm').

There's no entry for **faggot**—just then her mother opens the bedroom door to bring in her clean washing.

Barberry n. Bush with thorns, yellow flowers and red berries (of the Berberidaceae family).

As for **tapeworm**, it's totally disgusting.

Her mother leaves the room.

Between **peninsula** and **penitent** is '**penis** ['pēnis] n. Male mating organ', which cross-references '**rod** [rod] n. A thin straight metal bar | | A silver-tipped staff, or wand, insignia of vergers. | | A stick or bundle of sticks used for punishment. | | Male organ of copulation (rod, cylindrical, ending in the glans, where the urinary meatus opens). [Syn. PENIS.] | | *Nau.* The straight bar of an anchor, at one end of which is another transverse rod, at right angle to the arms or claws of the anchor.'

There's nothing for dick except '**Spotted dick** n. a

British steamed suet pudding containing dried fruit (usually currants) commonly served with custard. And **glans** only says it's Latin for 'acorn', or beechmast, brown nuts, pairs of which are enclosed in a prickly case.

All was not lost. There were still some people who didn't think she was a complete weirdo. Before her father's dick burst onto the scene, the carnival had been more or less fun. Rose had taken her over to climb in behind Christian in his dodgem car. Music, lights, throbbing and spinning, their bodies tossed every which way. Rose, sitting up front, toppled onto Christian and the lights were blinding and Solange's heart was pounding and in her belly it felt very hot and everything was spinning. 'Keep your hands inside!' yelled Rose.

Then she followed them to the shooting gallery. You have to be twelve or over to shoot but Rose looks older, she's already got boobs. A little white ball quivers in a wire cage. It looks like a terrified ghost. There's an ear-splitting explosion and the ball disappears.

Then they each buy some fairy floss and they have two francs, forty-five centimes left, and then her father flashes his dick.

She runs down the slope towards her street. The music fades. She has a pain in her belly but her legs are running by themselves, running faster than her. It's dark, the moon shines a white spotlight. There's no wind, the trees are still, stencilled shadows, and thousands of eyes are looking at her.

Someone is sitting on the terrace. It's Georges' girlfriend. She's asleep, tipped backwards in her chair. A camembert has melted all over the table and a big drip of it is hanging above her knees. It's really freaky. The hot air is like a perfectly adjusted volume control. Chairs, table, bottles of wine and Georges' girlfriend, trees, house, street: there's no more variation possible. Solange is the only one able to move, slowly, to activate her thorax in order to catch her breath.

All the doors are open. In her parents' bedroom, a bedside lamp has fallen over. It's hot, a yellow, murky heat. Her mother is on the bed, fully clothed, her face buried in the pillow. Obviously she's not asleep because her head turns beneath her hair and she says, 'Have you seen your father?'

Yes.

'Who was he with?'

With Georges.

Her mother's face is red and puffy. 'Only Georges? No one else?'

Yes.

Her mother reaches out her hand. 'What have you done to your hair? Have you cut your hair?' She pulls on a strand, like she's lengthening it. 'And your dress? Look at your dress!'

Along the hem of little red dogs, there are dark spots. On the pristine white, there are now more little red dogs.

Her mother's head falls back on the pillow. The church bell in the village sounds a single loud chime.

'Are you sure there was only Georges?'

Yes.

Under the electric light, her underpants are also full of dark spots, and the toilet paper has spots on it, too, bright red spots.

'Move over,' someone says. It's Georges' girlfriend, in front of her, gigantic, vomiting all of a sudden into the toilet. Her big body is all elbows and knees and she has her nose on the little dogs. 'You've got blood there,' she hiccups.

The dodgem cars must have broken something inside her belly.

'In Grade Six. And flat as a pancake,' her mother says to Georges' girlfriend. Drinking coffee among the oyster shells. The juice has run onto the tiles. 'I shouldn't have got white,' (apropos of the tiles).

She's not as flat as all that. Not compared to Nathalie, for example. When she cups her hand, the nipple reaches the palm. When she bends over, her breast almost fills the palm of her hand completely, but does that count?

Why don't roosters have hands? (Raphaël's riddle.) Because hens don't have breasts.

But 'hen' also means woman, just like 'hooker' means 'whore'. And 'pussy' is the name of what's between their legs.

At the swimming pool Raphaël grabbed her breasts from behind. She struggled but he wouldn't let go. Then he bragged about it to his friends.

Her mother and Georges' girlfriend are talking among the bits of shells and it doesn't seem to be about either Georges or her father, but about her. About the fact that they don't have any *napkins* and that the shops are still shut. Cotton wool, that would slip out, but a tampon would be too difficult, wouldn't it?

Georges' girlfriend doesn't think so. What's so difficult?

'She's clearly not your daughter,' says her mother. 'Grade Six. That's all we need. You've got the whole picture now.' She's smoking, studying the terrace as if it has fragmented before her eyes.

'So now she's a woman,' says Georges' girlfriend.

Her mother groans. 'And a woman when some brute has it off with her? And when she has a kid? You never stop becoming a woman. I'd certainly like to stop.'

'Or a face washer?' suggests Georges' girlfriend.

She's sitting in the shade with a *Peanuts* magazine. It's already hot. The terrace is rotating like a turntable in slow motion. The oyster shells stink. The juice is sticky on her feet.

'Go and get us some aspirin!' screams her mother.

As she gets up, it dislodges the face washer in her underpants. It's scratchy.

'In our day,' says Georges' girlfriend, seeing her all stiff and uncomfortable, 'we used to put a kind of nappy inside plastic pants. I'm not kidding.'

The two women watch the tablets dissolve in the glasses. It's as if the house was going to stay dirty forever.

She and her father leave on the pharmacy mission. (When he finally turned up, he had all his clothes on.)

Georges' girlfriend vomited last night.

'No way? I'm always telling your mother, you can't eat oysters in the months that don't have an "r" in them.'

May, June, July, August. July and August both have thirty-one days. Knuckles together, here is the church, index fingers pointed, here is the steeple, fingers splayed, open the doors and out come the people.

Papa, can you do this?

Hands clapped together, middle finger against middle finger, they are turning around the axis of a single weird finger.

'I'm driving, my little chickadee.'

The after-hours pharmacy is near the marina. You have to ring and be let in. There's a sign in the window that says: HAVE YOUR BLOOD PRESSURE TAKEN HERE.

'This is more your business than mine,' he says to the pharmacy woman with a wink.

'What do you need, Mademoiselle?'

The word tampon comes into her mind but she knows that's not it. Tampons are for her mother and for Georges' girlfriend. The word she's looking for is an ordinary word, like pumpkin, with another word that's more complicated, more academic, or gymnastic.

There's a poster with an anatomical model drinking a syrup for constipation. A green arrow goes straight down through his guts, without passing through the loops of the intestines.

'A packet of Modess,' her father ends up saying.

'We don't stock Modess. Stayfree?'

'Stayfree's fine. Now she'll stay free when she plays kiss chasey, ha, ha?'

He gives her a nudge.

She has *already lived through this scene*. It's because of the shame, but also because of the nudge, and the pharmacy woman, and the Stayfree and the staying free in kiss chasey: she's already seen this pharmacy woman, and now she'll remember this moment here between her father and the pharmacy woman for the rest of her life, she'll remember it, this moment that has come round again. Time has a hole in it. The past and the future have been connected like the mouth and the anus of the anatomical model—a hideous graft that short-circuits the twists and turns of the present.

And her father thinks he has to joke around with the woman for ages. It's just the way he gets on with people. It's his way of being polite. She'd like to pluck up the courage to ask if she can go to the toilet, to fix her underpants, and put in the *sanitary napkin*. She rocks from one foot to the other but the face washer stays stuck on one side. When she sits down in the car, a rush of warm liquid soaks her underpants.

They still have to go and buy flowers. Her father makes big gestures and speaks loudly and the florist piles everything left in her shop into the boot of the car: red and yellow roses, arum lilies, all sorts of coloured stuff, even gladioli.

'Don't make that face, you look like your mother. You've only got one life, my little chickadee.'

Does Lulu get this as well? She vaguely remembers something about underpants for a dog. For a female dog.

It's raining. The ground is steaming and opens up beneath the raindrops. Each drop releases the smell of the grass, the smell of the bitumen. If she got caught in a shower of rain on the way to school, how would she be able to run, with this package stuck between her legs? The world unfolds in shapes, noises and colours, but she's in a glass box, separated from it all.

'Hey, come and keep me warm!' Monsieur Bihotz calls out.

In bed with Monsieur Bihotz, the feeling of being inside glass continues. Those good strong smells, the big body of Monsieur Bihotz—the contrast is chilling. She pulls away from him. He grabs her by the foot, like a bear catching salmon. She pulls away again.

Those tadpole things inside men's dicks climb all over the sheets just like they swim around in the swimming-pool water, and they get inside girls. They swim up through the blood and make babies. Monsieur Bihotz doesn't seem to know about it, so it's up to her to be careful. Although there are also those strange times when he's writhing on the edge of the bed. Those times when he stands up, drapes himself in his dressing-gown and says, 'I stand on my dignity.'

When she finds him in the kitchen, armed with the coffee grinder, his head beneath the lampshade, his dressing-gown belted around him, she reminds herself that the distance she has just put between herself and him is the same distance that he sometimes insists on, as if he also, in his own way, was holding something back.

There's no MY, or MUMMY tattooed on Monsieur Bihotz's dick, no get fucked to anyone. There's nothing tattooed there at all. When she was little and Monsieur Bihotz gave her a bath, he always came in and had a piss. He pisses on the hydrangeas, too. He says it makes them go blue. He has two dicks. The one for pissing, and the other one. The other one is much bigger, the colour of a turkey's comb, like the canna lilies.

Monsieur Bihotz can spend whole days in bed. Not

the same way as her mother, who groans when you open the door and who needs absolute silence and complete darkness for her migraines. He has the shutters closed but the light turned on and he reads the newspaper, or listens to the radio, or goes as far as turning AC/DC on full bore, or he just lies there doing nothing, drinking lots of coffee. If he stays there too long, he tells her, 'I'm having a coffee meltdown.'

On one of the coffee meltdown days, Monsieur Bihotz was lying on his bed with the newspapers around him, his dressing-gown open, holding his big red dick in his hand. They looked at each other for what seemed like ages, but as long as she was looking at his eyes, she was not looking at his hand. Monsieur Bihotz's face became more and more mournful and thoughtful. Then he wrapped himself up in his dressing-gown and turned on his side and he started groaning, a bit like her mother.

Under the shower the water runs red. Every now and again a little black twisty thing pops out, like it's alive, caught in the current. A maxi-plus sanitary napkin for the night. 'The flow's heavier at night,' her mother said.

The engines of her father's plane are roaring on the tarmac. She knows the noise by heart. It gets more and more high-pitched, and then holds the note, loud. The plane flies just above the house. It's her father saying goodnight to her, on the weekends when he doesn't sleep at home. He veers off course especially for her. The lights traverse the black sky. They blink through the clouds, illuminating them, then they disappear.

She goes down the hall without turning on the light, careful where she places her feet, avoiding the lines between the tiles. Quietly she opens the door to her mother's room. She recoils because the colour is strange. It's sparkling like gold dust in the shadows. The glossy paper from the bouquets of flowers. Her mother has gathered all the flowers onto her bed and it looks like she's dead.

She gets some empty jam jars and fills them with water, and then she gives up, there are too many of them, it's so stupid, all these flowers her father bought.

'You'll live to see the last of the animals,' her father tells her. 'There'll only be useful animals left. Edible or ornamental. Rats and mosquitoes will survive. And seagulls.' Disgusted, he points his Dunhill towards the only thing still moving on the lake. 'Seagulls are indestructible. They breathe any old air, they float on any old bit of water, they eat anything and everything. They've even adapted to Clèves, and that's saying something.

'I wanted to live near the sea. But your mother didn't, because of the sea air. It rusts the shutters.

'The only thing left at the end of everything will be

cockroaches. Their shells are atomic bomb shelters. They can live under water and without food. The planet will be colonised by cockroaches crawling around in a desert. And you know what? Nothing much will have changed.

'I'll tell you something, my little chickadee. There are enough bombs in the silos to destroy the whole planet. Right now, in the Federal Republic of Germany alone, there is a thousand times more firepower than everything that blew up in the Second World War. Enough to make the Earth tilt on its axis. The dinosaurs disappeared all right. But in our case it'll be our own fault. The first time since the advent of life that we'll be part of a total self-destruction, not only of the species, but of its whole environment.' He relights his Dunhill while he stares at the lake.

'My big girl. My sweet chickadee.' His voice is raised, excited. He grabs her neck and jams her head under his bristly chin.

'Because, you see, under this lake, there's a silo. Not a corn silo, right? For a long time I was sure I'd see them, from up above. You can't see the Mayan designs when you're stuck on the ground like a stupid bastard. But as soon as you fly, you can see their runways. All the little bits you can't see from on the ground. I was sure I'd see the silos from the plane. But I've never seen them.'

So (she says) *there's a silo under the school. Or under our house.*

The lake ended in a geyser and a long missile emerged from it slowly, heavily, flawlessly spinning.

He took long crackling puffs on his cigarette. A moist smacking, an inhalation, then a long breath. A white wave that disappeared into his mouth and reappeared, paler.

Monsieur Bihotz likes animals too.

He always had the same urgent gesture, the same scalded look when he flicked the butt away.

'What are you talking about, chickadee. Monsieur Bihotz loves his dog.'

He likes hedgehogs. And ducks.

'I don't like animals. Do you get what I'm saying? But they exist. They're there. *For real.* Not like lapdogs or hens. Not like domestic animals.

'Can I teach you *one* thing in life? Can you listen to me? Listen to me for real? Monsieur Bihotz is just a granny with a lapdog. Like his mother. He took over from her.'

He got out of the car and walked along the edge of the lake. She didn't dare follow him.

He wasn't going to put Lulu in the Animal Protection Society, was he? she brooded.

He walked along the edge of the lake as if he was in an airport, surrounded by an invisible crowd, the only person with a precise destination, the only necessary person. Frowning, his eyes vacant, in permanent jet lag. A very adult adult.

She wanted to cry.

He got back in the car.

'We're not going to cry over a whale, one whale. We're

not going to bury it in the cemetery. We'd have to dig a hole as big as mother Bihotz.'

She laughed grudgingly.

'But if it's all the whales. A planet with only battery-farmed cows and abattoirs.'

She leans closer, her nose under his ribs, right where the breathing happens. The smoke goes in and out in time with the heartbeats: a large, complex and mysterious machine. She almost feels safe and she dozes off, weary.

'She's a little woman now,' her father says to Georges.

Georges looks at her. It's rare that adults don't know what to say, or rather it's normal—there's no possibility of conversation—but right now it's a familiar silence.

'Ah, yes,' her father says again, giving her his own special look too.

Georges' gaze is at the level of her breasts. Her nipples feel like they're on fire. As if two eyes were opening in her chest, agonising, blind and exposed to scrutiny.

They have a smoke before they leave and snigger together but it doesn't seem to be about her (her father is saying the pharmacy woman is *hot*).

Do all women get this? Her mother knows they do, enough to say 'fuck' when her skirt is stained—she quickly wets the bit of skirt with cold water and puts a soluble aspirin on it. It's a *trick*: the bubbles dissolve the blood. ('A tablet that can produce blood,' mother Bihotz used to say.)

'The first time I got mine, I was doubled over with pain,' her mother told her.

'It's not easy for boys either,' her father told her.

Do their dicks peel? She's heard about a boy who had to have an operation. Maybe it's like a snake: the skin doesn't grow, so it falls off in the process, and sometimes the sloughed skin stays stuck on the body? Perhaps they find bits of bleeding skin in their underpants? The idea that it's also difficult for boys helps a bit. Otherwise she's just too furious about the whole thing.

She squeezes her legs together as she walks. On the scale of pain, hers is fairly high: she's getting flashes of light in her eyes. The sanitary napkin is scratchy and keeps getting stuck. It's totally impossible to think about anything else.

Her father told her about Anne Chopinet, an engineering graduate of the Ecole Polytechnique. And Jacqueline Dubut who was the first woman pilot. One of his colleagues.

'You could be a pilot too, later on.'

Has Jacqueline Dubut got this? How can she concentrate on being a pilot? Did Anne Chopinet get it when she was in the 14 July military parade on the Champs-Elysées, carrying the Polytechnique's flag in front of everyone, a pad between her legs?

What does her teacher think about all this? How can she go to school with blood stuck there, and not knowing when it will stop (because she understands now: it's not going to stop).

'I've never seen him with a girl, never. And I mean that's ever since we moved in, when Solange was born and he was still in vocational training.'

Her father is drinking rosé with Georges on the terrace. She is drawing flowers in the condensation on the bottle. The droplets run down in long vertical stems.

'Whenever you've got a woman who won't let go of her son's balls, you'll always end up with a faggot. And if she dies, he's screwed for good.'

'I'm telling you,' says Georges, 'faggot or no faggot, he's pretty dodgy.'

'It's not an illness, being a faggot. And it's not something you're born with. It's more subtle than that. If you want to know what I really think,' her father continues, 'faggots are super-nice people, especially with kids. What on earth do you think he could possibly do to my daughter? He changed her nappies, just like he changed his mother's nappies. If he ever saw my daughter's pussy, all he'd see is a disgusting crack.'

She figures that, anatomically, it's quite logical; intellectually it makes sense; when she thinks clearly about it, it adds up:

men have a bit that hangs out, girls have a hole. They fit: one into the other.

In *A Life*, by Maupassant, she reads: 'All of a sudden she was gripped by a sharp pain; and she started groaning, writhing in his arms, while he possessed her violently.' Rose's mother is the one who makes them read it. André Sallenave says it goes in the belly button, but that's completely stupid. Except that, from what she's seen, like in old paintings, it will never fit. Not in hers anyway. It must hurt like hell, and there's no way she's being *possessed.* You possess an object or a house. Her intelligence is coming to her rescue.

She pushes the sentence round in all directions—'he possessed her violently'. Something clicks in her head and she's electrified: what she has between her legs will impel her to possess the world.

Concepción is having a party, a New Year's Eve party. The shutters are closed and the music is loud and Concepción's mother is smoking in the kitchen and her daughter is screaming at her in Spanish (apparently she has to stop coming into the living room). Everyone on the couches is kissing.

The music is saying: *everybody's gotta love some time, doum doum doum, everybody's gotta to love some time.* Not her. It will never happen to her. No one will kiss her. She'll never go out with anyone. *Doum doum doum.*

Raphaël Bidegarraï and Nathalie are kissing, with their

tongues, as if they were eating slugs out of each other's mouths. Concepción and one of the Lavinasse boys are at it. Even two young kids from Grade Five. Rose and Christian aren't kissing but they're sitting side by side and they're talking. And all the others are dancing, turning slowly, heads on each other's shoulders, arms around waists.

She is standing near the record player, rocking from one foot to the other. The music is enticing, but she's better off stopping herself, better off drinking a tenth glass of orange juice, than dancing all by herself with the invisible man.

Her father's dick, that's what they're talking about right now, everyone there is whispering into each other's hair about it. Her father's dick sticking out like his nose in the middle of his face. The world is spinning around this dick, microgroove by microgroove. *Everybody's gotta love some time*, in a spiral around the little spindle in the centre of the turntable, *everyone, everyone,* no one is looking at her but everyone is thinking about it. The little spindle finds its way into her retinas and covers the wobbling, impossible, white spot of her father's dick at the carnival at quarter to twelve under the church tower, to the sound of the oompahpah music, *everyone, everyone but you.*

The only thing left is to go into exile or to disappear. Far from this ridiculous village that is spinning right now, while it's stuck so ridiculously in this place on the Earth's crust. Far from her ridiculous body that no one would want even if she put it up for sale, even if she swapped it for a dog's body, no one would bid for it just to get the ball rolling.

'Mr and Mrs Fark have a son. What is his name? Roland. Roll and Fuck!' Raphaël Bidegarraï is telling the joke and Roland Boursenave is laughing so much that his face is all crinkled, his eyes are like a furious cat.

'Faggot!' hiccups Roland.

'Fuck you! Fuck you and the horse you rode in on!'

There's also that rhyme that she heard at the carnival: *Keen to do the deed, I'm all out of luck, All I need, all I need, Is the chance for a fuck.*

What is *fuck*?

Monsieur Bihotz is busy weeding the corner under the canna lilies, where the moss keeps coming back, like alien moss, no matter what he does, whether he digs it over, burns it, pours boiling water on it, covers it with salt, acid, bicarbonate of soda or weedkiller.

In the *Nouveau Larousse universel* there is just a line space between **fry** and **fudge**.

'It's a very vulgar word,' Monsieur Bihotz explains.

Just what she would have got from her parents.

'Especially from the mouth of a young girl,' he adds.

Up until now, when he spoke about her, he said 'a little girl'. She remembers a fairy tale in which, instead of words, pearls came out of the mouth of a princess. She can feel the little hard beads, like cherry pips, *ptt, ptt, ptt,* between her lips.

She sits on his knees so they can play Giddey up, Horsey and he can jump her up in the air.

Today he says, 'Stop.'

What does fuck mean?

'Stop.'

She puts her arms around his neck, watching out for his teeth, for that scary wolf thing he does with his teeth.

But Monsieur Bihotz gets up; he's strong and heavy and she nearly falls. He goes into his bedroom and she thinks he's going to have a coffee meltdown. But no, he comes out again with a little cup and ball game in his hand. He holds the ring delicately between his thumb and index finger, an egg about to crack.

'This is fucking,' he explains. He throws the ring up in the air, and in precisely one go, only one, it lands on the pin.

Sometimes dogs stick their muzzles between her legs. She pushes them away, her hand on their hard little skulls. They are like small children, harmless and a bit crazy.

Another summer day in the hills outside town. There's a pack of dogs. They come and go as if the road belongs to them, roving around in a world without humans, a world on four legs and itinerant ears. She is invisible and odourless, she calls to them but they don't answer to names anymore.

She is just an obstacle between them and what's under a tree over there.

Lulu is under the tree. Big Yellow is on top of Lulu. Some of the other dogs want to climb on top of Lulu but Big Yellow growls and bares his teeth. They are all panting and whimpering. Most of them have a big, glistening, red dick under their bodies. The dogs are circling, stalking, and Big Yellow won't stop, and the panting and the tongues, and the paws are scraping on the ground and on top of Lulu, and everywhere the same staring, glittering eyes. Lulu groans and her back legs give way. She sits but keeps struggling to get up. Big Yellow is bigger than her, and the smaller dogs have a go at her with their little dicks, and Lulu looks like she wants it and doesn't want it, swept away in her panting by something that has possessed them all and has lodged itself in all their eyes—it's like a giant eye under the tree.

She throws stones at them. She kicks them. She screams but nothing happens, they continue to be dogs, without her, with whatever it is under the tree that sweeps them up and envelops them, something terrifyingly adult, ancient, something that is no longer about playing a game.

There's no sign of dogs in Rose's house. Behind the hedge, there are afternoon teas with buns, music and elegant boots. There is no blood, no pubic hair and no dicks. It's as if Rose lives in a different housing development, in a parallel world, to which she has no access, even though it is right there within earshot. You can hear the loud splashing and the squeals of summer, and Rose's bubbly laughter, and the high-pitched voices of the boys from school. The gunshot explosions when they jump in the pool.

In her house, the shifting shadows, and the doorbell that tinkles, without the wind.

She's in pain and it won't go away. Her mother makes an appointment with the gynaecologist.

Kilometres of ripe corn. An advertisement with a woman holding a bottle between her breasts. The incandescent white of the co-op silos. The open windows let in four blasts of scorching air that whip around their heads with a roar.

'Your reproductive system is gearing up,' says the gynaecologist. She makes her lie down naked on a metal bed and open her legs. She should relax, it's a *virgin speculum*. She feels a cold pain and she wants to close her legs but the gynaecologist tells her that the examination will soon be over, oohh but it's so tight in there.

As she writes out the prescription, she talks with her mother about the arrival of the holiday-makers. About Georges' girlfriend who's expecting a baby.

Her mother rents two deckchairs on the promenade. They lie there; her mother's in a bikini and she's in shorts. Last year she was making sandcastles down there in the sand. Her mother has put on her dark glasses; her gaze and her mouth are set in the direction of the invisible distance. Blinding light. The hotels and casinos are cut out against the sky like big blue stickers.

She puts on her Vuarnet sunglasses, a present from her father. The red-and-white bathing boxes, the strip of sand, the bodies, the sea. The boys jump off the low wall with their surfboards under their arms. Their legs in skin-tight black pants, muscly torsos, long blond hair, creatures from a different species, unattainable. The air they breathe is not the air she struggles to get into her lungs.

The women on the beach, all with different bodies, have they got it? Not now, not right away (or perhaps with a tampon), but in general, in their everyday lives? How is it possible for women to get this thing, and for everyone to act as if nothing was the matter? It must be dangerous to be bleeding with sharks around. Anyway, you're not supposed to swim because the salt water triggers haemorrhages.

Can I have an ice-cream?

Her mother turns to her. 'From now on, everything you eat will go straight to your hips.' She flings herself back onto her lilo. Still fed up, she yanks down the straps of her bikini top so she won't get any marks.

The horizon is empty. No shark fin, no whale spout, no giant octopus. And yet, right now, in this very ocean, in these very molecules of water, unheard-of beasts are coexisting with swimmers.

It's her turn to tilt her head in the direction of the

sky. Her lilo is whirling towards the yellow disc of the sun. Something is unwinding and rewinding, superimposing other skies over the sky, something that is slowly tipping her into empty space.

Time is a long, wavy, blue ribbon, with wide stripes for the years to come—middle school, Grade Six, Year Seven, Year Eight. The stripes get narrower towards high school and become pale and blurred towards the year 2000 mark. Then they get even thinner, less and less clear: a fleecy, infinite sky.

She is watching a western with Monsieur Bihotz. A squaw is tied up in the dust. Cowboys with hats on, yelling, riding horses that are missing her by a hair's-breadth. The ropes wound around her thin body are tied tight across her fringed dress. She would like to be able to stop the picture, turn it into a photograph and keep it forever, to look at it when she's alone.

The squaw has been hitched onto a horse; the cowboy whacks the horse's rump with the flat of his hand, yee-ha! It's not the TV she'd need to be able to stop, but the galloping inside her, this horse which is gaining speed and thrashing along, endlessly thundering. How to react to being swept away like that?

Or perhaps it's all about Christian? In an issue of *Jours de France*, there is a drawing of a woman lying down and the caption says: 'Dreaming about him, an exquisite shuddering overwhelms her.' That's exactly it. Dreaming about Christian, an exquisite shuddering overwhelms her. She can spend ages dreaming about Christian.

About how she will go on outings with Christian. About how their house will be (with a fireplace). About the names of their children (Coralie, Aurélie, Athéna, Jennifer). She snuggles up against Bihotz, her arm around his waist, her head in the hollow of his pillow, her arm tenderly draped over the bolster of the bed.

She rubs the flat of her palm just below the hard bit, where her bony part stops, at the top of the soft flesh like puff pastry, thick and hot. She stays on the edge of it. She doesn't push and especially not lately when there's been blood there. She rubs, in little circles. A knot swells and tightens, a mechanism that perks up simply and effectively, at the junction of the bones and the flesh, as if the skeleton was designed to carry at its centre this budding plump heart. Images flash past, the squaw on the horse, and a naked woman, on her knees, in her mother's *France-Loisirs* shopping catalogue, on the 'adults' page. The pressure becomes almost unbearable, she holds herself back as much as she can, to let it erupt in one go—then, a familiar numb drowsiness. She wipes herself with the sheet and lets the vision of a horse carry her off to sleep.

*

Rose invites her to the beach with her three cousins from Paris.

She's discovered the relaxing sensation of being covered only in skin, dry and dependable right into its creases, a sealed bag that moves around with the body and that you can wash in the sea, and undress in the sun.

The two mothers have lowered their voices in an alarming way. She swears they're talking about it, and Rose's mother gives her a sweet, anxious smile.

Actually there's a car problem: Rose and her mother and the three cousins, and her as well. Whoops, it's too many for the Renault 16.

'I'm going to ask the Bihotz lad, he's so obliging, the Bihotz lad solves all our problems.' Her mother's sentences skate over the world. Right there in the narrow house, she seems to engage in a short ballet sequence followed by a few acrobatic moves.

'What fun it will be in Monsieur Bihotz's van!' chants Rose's mother, revealing herself to be another champion skater, international standard, in her red boots.

Even though they were ready at eleven o'clock (ten o'clock at the latest, Monsieur Bihotz had said), the beach already looks like the quilt on mother Bihotz's bed: little squares of colour butting up against each other. 'How long did it take us, Monsieur Bihotz?'

Monsieur Bihotz would rather stay on the promenade. 'Come with us,' Rose's mother insists, 'the more the merrier.'

She points to the tiny spot where she thinks they'll all fit.

'How great that Maman could bring us to the beach,' says Rose (and she and her mother do that annoying thing of kissing each other on the mouth, a little peck).

'We,' says one of the cousins, the oldest, it must be Sixtine 'don't have the sea, but we have the Seine.'

When my father flies his plane to Paris, he has dinner on the Champs-Elysées.

'You're so cute,' says Rose's mother, in a funny voice, like she's apologising for her.

'My father is a radiologist,' says Meredith. 'Do you have a swimming pool?'

The three Parisiennes have spread out sarongs, Rose and her mother have mats, and she has her Snoopy bath towel. Monsieur Bihotz has brought out a ghastly floral towel, the one from the downstairs washbasin. Even though she sits as far away from him as possible—perhaps it's because of the fabric, the terry towelling—it still seems to her as if she *smells* like him.

He is wearing his blue shorts and has kept his T-shirt on, which is a mercy. He's sweating profusely, and his little towel barely extends beyond his buttocks, like blotting paper. She avoids looking in his direction.

The triangles over Rose's bust are more filled out than she would have imagined. As for Sixtine, who has kept on her pedal-pushers and is wearing a very pretty bikini top, her breasts are almost as big as Rose's mother's, but she's in Year Eight. Rose lifts up the elastic band on her buttock to compare tans. Sixtine coats her sisters in the new Ambre Solaire Totale. She says that monoi oil doesn't do anything except make you smell of coconut. 'Coconut, coconut!' yells Alma, roaring with laughter, but she's in Grade Two. 'You've got to peel,' contradicts Rose's mother, 'that way your skin gets used to it.' She undoes her bikini top so she's topless.

Monsieur Bihotz heaves his big body as upright as possible, so he doesn't tip onto anyone, and says something inaudible. So she repeats it for him, as if she was translating: *He's going to buy an ice-cream.* Monsieur Bihotz goes red and repeats his sentence louder, too loud, like he's speaking to the whole beach—so loud that the people next to them turn round to listen.

'I'm going to buy some ice-creams.'

'Not for me,' says Sixtine. 'Méré, Alma, do you want one?'

'That's so kind of you, Monsieur Bihotz,' gushes Rose's mother. 'Wait, I'll get my purse.'

But Monsieur Bihotz has got his stupid Roman-emperor look, standing on his dignity again, he's already heading off in those ridiculous shorts, stepping over the mats. Now they have to yell out their flavours. Two scoops of vanilla for Rose's mother. Apricot-pear for Alma. Cherry-nougat for Méré. Licorice if there's no nougat. She runs after him. Pistachio-chocolate for Rose. Same for her.

That's going to cost you a fortune.

And he's already paid for the petrol.

'You can talk about that when you've got your own money.'

He doesn't head for The Ice-cream Palace, but for Monsieur Lopez's truck. Monsieur Lopez recognises him and lets them both go to the head of the queue. They chat. The sun's shining. 'You came together?' Monsieur Bihotz waves his arm, but Monsieur Lopez sees the four cousins and Rose's mother. 'You don't muck around, do you, Bibi?' (Apparently Bibi is Monsieur Bihotz's nickname.)

Bibi buys vanilla-strawberry gelati for everyone (but a double vanilla for Rose's mother). By the time they've stepped over the crowd again, the ice-creams are already melting. They have to stop and lick them, quickly, quickly. And they're laughing just like at home, as if they were alone in the sunshine, as if (she reminds herself) he was her big brother, say, and not this gawky yeti.

'It's absolutely fabulous here,' says Sixtine, refusing an ice-cream. 'You've got everything in the one place. In Paris you have to go for miles to get the best ice-cream, and then even further to get the best tea. Here everything's in the same street. Do you have a Cacharel boutique?'

Rose's mother suggests they go for a swim, but Sixtine, looking wounded and pouting coyly, says she is 'indisposed'. The announcement is met with respectful silence. Rose's mother gets up. She hops up and down because the sand is boiling. Her breasts are round and white like two scoops of vanilla ice-cream, with pink creases from the raffia mat.

'Are you coming with us, Monsieur Bihotz?'

Monsieur Bihotz wiggles his feet and then shakes his head.

'But Monsieur Bihotz, you can go swimming, can't you?'

Rose and her cousins burst into hysterical laughter.

Rose's mother swims off straight away with a perfect freestyle stroke, diving under the breakers as if, between her and America, the ocean was nothing but a silly nuisance; off she shoots, further and further, released from her boots, which are right here, stinking in the sun. Rose and Sixtine are whispering, their hair mingling. Monsieur Bihotz has turned over onto his front, his arms pressed against his sides, his mammoth feet almost touching Rose's bum. Doing his best to distribute his massive body, he occupies as circumspectly as possible his five billionth share of the Earth's crust: right here, on some burning sand.

She'd like to swim off straight away, like Rose's mother, into that watery element. She'd like to believe that between her and the sea there is some kind of transcendental pact that excludes the rest of humanity. Despite the fact that she scarcely knows how to swim, however, it seems to her as if she should stay and rescue Monsieur Bihotz here, on dry land. Something about the points of this triangle, Rose, Sixtine and Monsieur Bihotz, demands her urgent attention.

He's got that dazed look about him, like when he's

having a coffee meltdown. Quivering, a slight shudder, as if he was trying to hold himself still.

Rose and Sixtine are red in the face from suppressed laughter. Sixtine doesn't say anything, and when Rose lets forth she hides under her sarong.

'He's got an erection,' hisses Rose. Solange is also keen to bury herself in her raffia mat, but is less successful.

Sixtine whispers a story that happened to her in the metro—she's addressing Rose, but you can hear her over the sound of the sea and the children screaming—about a man jammed right up against her and she didn't know if it was his *briefcase* or some other hard thing, that's the trouble with public transport. She complained to her mother who now takes her everywhere by car. 'It's disgusting,' sympathises Rose, 'it's vile, how horrible. I'll never ever take the metro!'

'Monsieur Bilost!' Sixtine suddenly calls out. 'Monsieur Bilost!'

Monsieur Bihotz twists his head around.

'Monsieur Bilost, would you like to play volleyball with us?'

Rose looks at Sixtine as if she was magnificently mad. But her mother comes back, grabbing a T-shirt to dry herself quickly. Beneath her Bo Derek plaits, her brilliant white teeth reflect the sun's glare. She gives a wet wave to a lifeguard.

Monsieur Bihotz goes for a swim, finally. By himself.

On the way back, they doze, stuck in the overheated shade of the van. The sun's rays beat on the rear-vision mirrors and two square patches of light bounce off the inside panels.

'What sort of music do you have?' Rose's mother asks, leaning on Monsieur Bihotz as she rummages among the cassettes, bumping against him and laughing and yelling, 'YOU CAN SEE THE PYRENEES, GIRLS!' over the top of *look for your happiness everywhere-ere, say no to this selfish wo-orld.*

'Aren't they beautiful, those silos,' she continues, 'typical of between-the-wars architecture, look at that stepped roof, right out of the housing co-operative style, the building itself expresses hope, social cohesion.'

The sun slips from one rear-vision mirror to the other, landscape, road, sky, Pyrenees, swirling slowly inside the van, a crest of jagged light glints with each corner taken, illuminating the forehead of Rose's mother and becoming that forehead, those eyes, then leaving them in the shade while her thighs come alight and the glovebox and the whole windscreen and some of the reflected faces, the two youngest cousins asleep in the back, Rose daydreaming, Sixtine annoyed because it's so hot, Rose's mother delighted by a sudden passing thought, Monsieur Bihotz whose lips are moving in time with the song—and someone else, the youthful, round, red face of a girl sitting in the middle, stunned and staring, narrow shoulders and a blue bathing costume over two pointed nipples, looking in the rear-vision mirror between the six other faces to see who it could possibly be there in the van, with them as well, as well as the six of them and Monsieur Bihotz, until a shaft of sunlight straight from the west shatters the image and she understands—her blue bathing costume, her little breasts, her face, Solange, her, Solange, me in the rear-vision mirror calling myself Solange and coming back from the beach in my ten-year-old body, me at the foot of the Pyrenees waiting for the future.

II

DOING IT

A few summers later, the same summer over again. Her breasts a bit bigger. Raphaël wants to finger Nathalie; Nathalie tells her and asks, should she let him?

I don't know if you should, she replies casually.

They are playing Mastermind. It's a rustic sun, yellow and green, hopeless. She imagines slimy fingers, fingers stuck up like when boys make rude gestures. Stay cool. Don't look uptight.

'Do you think you're still a virgin after it?' Nathalie presses the point.

Give an opinion. One finger, that's smaller than a dick, isn't it?

Nathalie has brought homemade cookies for her. Her nails are black with chocolate. No way in the world she's eating those cookies.

'I'd wet my pants,' admits her cookie-baking friend.

Nathalie has already done so many cool things, tongue-kissing, letting them feel up her breasts and all that. If she gets wet, does that *also* mean she's scared? And how many holes are there altogether? In the end, can you get into all of them? Do *boys* get into all of them? Do boys get wet, and scared, too?

At the fountain that used to be a public washing place, a group of Saint-Jacques pilgrims are drinking water out of their scallop shells.

Why? Her father gets to fly to Paris; why does she have to live here?

Language hovers above the house like a cloud. All it needs is one word for a disaster to strike them, a catastrophe, a Boeing aeroplane in pieces.

But Clèves is very pretty, says her father. Its eighteenth-century chateau. Its half-timbered houses. Its marina, its windsurfing. Its chestnut cakes. Its pewter-ware shops. Its statue of the Virgin Mary. Its scenic rock that you can climb on.

Its pharmacy woman, someone adds—no, that can't be right. It's the voice in her head, saying things accumulated in the cloud.

Under the arches there's Christian on his moped, Rose and Sixtine, Nathalie and Delphine (the one who lives in the chateau), and Raphaël Bidegarraï. Raphaël is smoking a cigarette, which is pretty gutsy right in the middle of the village. He's got a thin black moustache and pimples. Christian is giving him a hard time because he's going out with Peggy Salami.

'A hole is a hole and my dick can't see,' he retorts.

Sixtine is wearing 501s with a military belt under an XXL T-shirt, sleeves rolled-up; as if her little body had had to make do with old men's clothes, from which her tanned, thin arms emerge, all the more graceful. Her ballerina flats under the frayed hem of her jeans make her feet look like they're barely there. All legs, this girl would walk on air: no toes, no nails, no weight. And there she is, Solange, in a tracksuit, on a bike, in huge sneakers that aren't even Adidas…

According to Rose, Sixtine has done it. Can you tell from looking at her? Something about her body, about her attitude? It's probably the opposite: it's *because* she has that look—classy—that she's been able to do it.

The pilgrims are mesmerised. They can't be looking at her, not the red-faced village girl—or are they sneaking looks? What's the matter with that old guy? Has she got something on her face? Any minute now he'll be taking her photo, making an offer for her mother's pewter and scoffing chestnut cake.

'You look hot on that bike!' he shouts at her in front of everyone.

She turns even redder. Embarrassing. So embarrassing.

And not far away, just when she's reached the steep path where there are always dogs, who should she see but the other lunatic with his scallop shell from a pack of frozen Coquilles Saint Jacques. In an attempt to regain her composure, she starts patting the dogs.

'You're kind to the dogs,' says the pilgrim, 'so what about me, don't you want to be kind to me?'

She rushes home to Monsieur Bihotz; too bad about self-possession.

Rose has done it, too. In England. 'A guy, you don't know him.' She refuses to tell her any more, for the sake of decency. 'We're like sisters.' But she told Nathalie, who tells Solange that Rose was gritting her teeth waiting for it to stop. That at first it wouldn't go in at all. Then it went in all at once and that was *so* horrible. Like her insides were being torn apart. And then there was blood everywhere. So much that she had to run to the showers, wrapped in a towel, and it was *pissing* blood. His dick was covered in blood, too. He cleaned himself up and told her through the door that it was okay, that he wasn't the one who was bleeding. She bled like that for two days without daring to tell anyone. Then it stopped but she was still in pain. She wondered whether she should go to the hospital to get some stitches or something, but she couldn't talk about it; she was in England, after all.

'Rose must be frigid,' Nathalie reckons.

Concepción says that if you're in love it doesn't hurt as much. And Delphine says that if you have light periods, you don't bleed or hardly at all.

Rose's English exchange student is called Terry and he's here for two weeks. He's a creature from outer space. He's eight inches taller than the rest of the village, and his hair is so blond, his eyes so pale, that you'd think he was visiting from the set of *Village of the Damned*. She practises pronouncing *Terry*, the soft 'T', the very soft 'r'. *Terry*, with as much smoothness and elegance as possible, she allows the air to slip between the two syllables, with just a faint hint of the final 'i'. She practises in front of the mirror, *Terry*. Then she says *Christian. Terry. Christian.*

How to choose? *No, Terry, no,* she murmurs into the mirror, refusing to be kissed. Then she's holding Christian's hand for ages, agonising with him over this impossible dilemma. She kisses her reflection, *Christian* is the one, *Terry* is the one. She kisses the back of her hand, then the inside of her arm, it's warmer, more realistic, using her tongue, wrapping her other arm around her waist.

She's allowed to stay at the carnival until half past twelve (the extra half hour on condition that she stays with Rose and Nathalie the whole time). She told her mother she's sleeping at Monsieur Bihotz's place, and told Monsieur Bihotz she's sleeping at home.

Rose lets Terry walk three feet in front of them. She rolls her eyes theatrically: 'He's really good-looking, but he's so clingy!'

He whips around when they laugh: 'Excusez-moi?'

They're laughing so hard they have to stop under a plane tree. The guy smoking under the plane tree goes to their high school and he's a bass player and he blows a kiss to Rose and Nathalie.

She just puts her hands in the pockets of her jeans. But that looks dumb. Arms dangling, that's even worse. She looks at her shoes, her summer pair, La Redoute mail-order, brown to go with everything.

The English exchange student also has weird clothes but perhaps that's just because he's English. If he's caught a plane to get all the way over here, he should be able to afford some fashionable shoes. The more she looks at him, the better looking he gets. Better built, more *manly* than the boys from around here, even if he seems a bit shy. And a movie star's face. That look of anguish and sadness.

She looks at his mouth, *Terry*, his upper lip. He always looks like he's about to speak, but then he doesn't. That lip keeps quivering—it's an unusual shape, straight across, without that fold that ordinary mouths have—she watches it stretching like that, a hint of downy blond fuzz, sliding over impeccable teeth, hiding them, revealing them…She couldn't care less about Rose and Nathalie, she couldn't care less about the bass player talking to them, she could keep looking forever at the English exchange student's upper lip, *Terry's* upper lip.

'Bunch of faggots.' Raphaël Bidegarraï greets them all. 'Shit, you're starting to look hot.' He tries to touch her bum, to give her a special greeting, but she hops sideways and Nathalie cackles, 'You should have seen your face!' What face, what face was she making? A hurt face like her mother's? The face of a stuck-up bitch—when Raphaël is just having a laugh. He's really nice when you get to know him.

There was that time at the swimming pool in Grade Five when he held her against the side and stuck his hands on her breasts and the shock paralysed her—she's replayed the scene a thousand times, a good kick would have got him off her—and it's the same Raphaël there in front of her now, with those same hands, one nonchalantly holding a smoke, the other in the pocket of his jeans. His appreciative gaze, his specialist's gaze. Apparently he goes out with the bombshells at high school.

'What're you doing?' he asks her, tilting his chin to exhale the smoke.

She hesitates: what's she doing in the future (going into Year Ten), or what's she doing there, in the present, right now, being a girl, at the carnival, this same carnival where her father flashed his dick—what's she doing?

She decides to reply seriously, sincerely (she's noticed that to sound sincere about what you think makes you seem interesting). She leans in to him: 'I'd like to go out with the English guy.'

Raphaël looks at Terry. Then at her. He gives his verdict. 'You can only go out with someone who's in the same league as you.'

Does he really think he's as good-looking as the girls he goes out with? It's too late to answer.

Who do you think you are?

You think it's only about looks?

The same league as your bullshit?

Like when you were going out with Peggy Salami?

She has no sense of repartee. She is hopeless.

Christian says it fucks you up, gives you cancer, but in the end he takes one and Nathalie does too and so does she. Her father has already made her take a drag of a Dunhill, to put her off. She lets her hand hang down along the seam of her jeans. Smoking—she's been doing it all her life. No one coughs.

Some children are squirting them with a water pistol. Nathalie yells at them. On the merry-go-round other kids are fighting over the plane that goes up and down.

And then this amazing thing happens: Terry gives her a sign that he wants to talk with her. They sit down away from the others. Terry seems to be looking for his courage and his words, it's not easy in Fwench. Firecrackers explode, he jumps out of his skin, they both laugh. He says Wose something—she can't hear with all this noise.

Rose is the last person she wants to talk about—but let him talk as much as he likes, let his upper lip go up and down, 'u' pronounced *ou*, the warm breath exhaled by those lips that are not closing—let him talk, let him talk about Wose who is cwuel and ignaws him in the stweet, in the what, in the stweet.

Loud thuds from inside the booth they're leaning against, like neighbours complaining. Heavy neighbours. It's the animal enclosure, part of the circus that comes back every year for the carnival. Madame Bihotz used to take her along when she was little. There was an old lion the same colour as the beige carpet in her parents' bedroom, a woolly camel, and an uncomfortable-looking sea lion. Animals so displaced (what on earth is that tewwible noise?) that they probably see this village (does Wose talk to you about me at all?) as just another moment of disillusion in the false promise of a round trip back home—but it's never the savannah, the steppe, the desert, or the sea. She's got to do it—Wose, Wose, the only thing coming out of his mouth is Wose—just concentrate for a minute—kiss a boy, go out with a boy, him or another one, him rather than another one. And whatever happens, this Terry will leave the village, and whatever happens—she reminds herself suddenly—she too will leave the village one day.

Air rushes into her lungs. Air from way beyond the

carnival and the circus and the clouds, air from the steppes and from the Milky Way.

Do you want to go out with me? she asks him clearly and super-comprehensibly, much more clearly and comprehensibly than she would have thought credible (cwedible).

'Go out,' he repeats, 'yes, go out, gwate idea.'

He stretches to the full British extent of his height, she stretches her neck giraffe-like, but nothing happens.

They are going out.

They are going out of what? Of the carnival? Of the village? He's walking fast, she scurries behind him.

But she's pretty sure it's the same in English: you say *go out* for kissing.

They're going past Gym Tonic. Past the Cheap Carpet outlet. Past the junkyard and the gravel pit. The *out* is becoming gigantic, the misunderstanding endless, the *out* spreads from the edge of the village, encompasses the silos, the forest and the hills, and unfolds onto the black sky and the horizon.

They're walking, he's in front, she's behind. The fields disappear under a grey fog that sweeps over the road and swirls around their calves, as if the planet was vaporising and then scattering into the night. *Whoo ooh* from the owls in the black trees. The green and pink sign of Milord's comes into view, the top hat and cane in neon lights.

She trots up to him quickly, sweating, *whoo ooh*. Should she fall into his arms? Or feign an illness, low blood sugar? The Milord shakes his cane and his hat. Some sort of creature is rustling the shrubbery, a fox, perhaps? She grabs his arm, he trips, they bump into each other. 'Tewwibly sowwy, you all wight?'

She gives up. *We might as well go to Milord's*. She makes up her mind for both of them. It's as if she's done this all her life, like smoking.

Girls get in for free, but not boys. She lets him sort that out and orders a Pineapple-Malibu cocktail. Hardly anyone there. A dance floor, empty, and a disco ball turning.

He orders. *One beer*, she translates. It's exhilarating to be in a nightclub. And to be with someone, to be able to let the three guys there think she's going out with this stud. The music is super-loud. She has a bit of a dance, glass in hand, sipping on the straw. The dance-floor tiles light up like in the 'Billie Jean' video.

'What's your name?'

Charlotte.

Her favourite first name for the last few weeks.

'Whaa…?'

Charlotte!

From a song she loves. In the school toilets she teases her hair like Michael Jackson. And Nathalie draws under her eyes with black kohl, just like he does.

'Tricky name! Where are you from?'

From Clèves!

'And you're not at the carnival?'

It sucks!

'The carnival sucks?'

Yeah, it sucks!

That makes him laugh, she doesn't know why.

He must be about twenty-five. Pretty ordinary (her mother would say). But muscly under his wolf-print T-shirt (Monsieur Bihotz has the same one). He's a fireman, he yells, he and a couple of workmates are having a bucks' night.

'I'm getting married tomorrow!'

Congratulations!

Having Terry over there, at the bar, gives her a feel for repartee. Or at least for an appropriate response.

'Is that your guy?'

No!

The fireman shoots a final glance at the English boy and yells again, at the top of his voice, 'Gimme a kiss, to celebrate?'

That's it. It's going to happen. As long as the nightclub doesn't burn down, as long as Monsieur Bihotz doesn't turn up wielding an axe, as long as her father doesn't land in the middle of the dance floor, finally, she is going to *go out with a guy*.

And maybe more than that, maybe she'll go further, because two hands grab her buttocks, pull her against the wolf on the T-shirt, two hands hoist her up firmly, not bothering about the rhythm of the music anymore, a bigger and bigger face is pushing down at her, the wily wolf and the mouth on mouth, dry and hot, a bit bristly, she opens her mouth and the hands squeeze her and an amazing pressure radiates through her cunt, coursing through her buttocks and her groin, her mouth melting too, and her tongue penetrating the mouth of the huge body, which responds with a hard, pointed tongue, he's not kissing the way she would like but who cares, the pressure fills her whole body and a hand lets go of her buttocks and slides under her T-shirt, the nipple on one breast is pinched and pulled, the enormous pressure stars to whirl, needs to become some other vibrant and shining thing and her own hands start to explore and grab and hunt and investigate—'Oh Charlotte,' says the huge body.

Not really in ecstasy; more like reining in a horse. 'Oh Charlotte,' like she is a filly.

She pulls herself together. A bit of decorum called for. Boogie with the fireman. He smells of sweat and cigarette smoke, she has a syrupy taste in her mouth. Blaring music and the dance floor flashing in time. He says, 'Are you slack?' or perhaps it was 'I'll give you a smack'. She can't hear properly so they sidestep over to a pillar ('lean back'?) where it's pretty dark ('new track'?) and one of the fireman's hands is inside her underpants ('what're you like in the sack?') and then one of the fireman's fingers, it's amazing, slides into her vagina ('ah, it's wider than a crack'?). She'll be able to use tampons.

But it's kind of uncomfortable. She twists around to

extricate herself, muffled words, he kisses her and pushes his finger in further, his hand stuck to her sucking wet cunt, uncomfortable but too bad, if that's what he wants, let him keep going—right now, like this—she doesn't dare take the initiative again, so she holds him by the shoulders, he rubs the lump in his jeans against her, he opens his fly and just then the *boum boum boum* of 'Billie Jean' starts up.

It's a sign! Her second favourite song. They're having a special moment here, her first kiss, dedicated to Michael Jackson *boum boum boum*! This song makes her feet and hips move *irresistibly. I can't help it!* she yells, laughing, writhing away, dancing, but he holds onto her, grabs onto her, he shouts something, it sounds like 'what the fuck' ('come out to my truck' 'get down 'n' suck') and his dick sticking out of his jeans, blinking beneath the lights and shadows.

Billie Jean is not my lover *boum boum boum.*

'I couldn't find you anywhere,' says Terry, with almost no accent. 'What did you do with that guy, what the fuck did you do with that guy,' he's just about shaking her.

He's a pompier, she pleads, there's no harm in being with a *pompier*, how do you say *pompier* in English? Are people looking at them? Is someone going to make fun of her? There's no one on the dance floor, four or five figures at the bar, and the fireman has disappeared.

Trees and fields. The *boum boum boum* is getting weaker, *whoo ooh* in the branches, a stifling night. Her head is still resounding with the bass line. Perhaps it's the

Pineapple-Malibu. Her underpants go stiff as she scampers behind Terry, it feels weird.

It must be three o'clock in the morning by the time they get back to the village and what's left of the carnival. Christian is sitting slumped against his moped; apparently he vomited. Rose went home furious, 'the worst night of her life, she's going to give you hell' (warns Nathalie, whose kohl is smudged and whose parents are there, with Georges, Papa's mate, at the drinks stand, which is still open). The band is playing 'Que je t'aime', the singer has hair like Boy George. She doesn't want Georges to see her (her parents' Georges).

Terry has disappeared. Nathalie is talking to some guys. Couples are dancing slowly. Clusters of people wander around. The trees are swaying. Wires are hanging from the branches. The sky is stencilled sheet metal. It becomes impossible to go home. Impossible to go to bed.

She can still feel in her groin the sensation of the fireman's hands, and his bristly face and the smoky taste, and right then and there, in front of the unmoving merry-go-round, it hits her—it's all tight, burning, wet—at the mere thought of his hands and mouth, there's a gripping sensation between her legs. Standing up, gaping, stunned, remembering what happened an hour ago, feverishly remembering—the sky becomes grey in the east and she's back there, at Milord's, glued to this unknown body. She has to be back there, not at Milord's, not with that man, but inside that thing at the centre, right now, that moment when everything's ablaze.

The band has stopped playing. The musicians are carrying heavy black cases. A man and a woman are dancing through the silence, hanging off each other. The shutters have come down on the drinks stand and her father is there on a chair. Not in the plane or in Paris but there. A female figure is sitting on his knees. It's not her mother or the pharmacy woman. It's the singer who looks like Boy George.

He tries to stand up but can't. He yells that he's dreaming. He yells at her to go to bed and asks in a really loud voice what the fuck she's still doing there. He yells where've you been, what the fuck is she doing out this late, where has she been?

By midday the next day the world is back to the way it was. Hours have sixty minutes and are marked by the ringing of the church bell, ladle-banging on the Clèves mess tin. A cow moos, the yellow air sticks like jelly. The thermometer reads 32 degrees, the horizontal lines are trembling on the hillsides.

Monsieur Bihotz came to check on her at eight in the morning; he thought they'd go fishing. 'He hasn't noticed that you're growing up,' says her mother (on the phone, she's at the shop). 'Keep the shutters closed, so the house stays cool.'

Scratchy lips, those hands, and the touch of a stranger. *My first kiss*, she repeats it to herself, *my first kiss*. A little bit of this incredible event settles in these three words, my first kiss, my first kiss. 'Daydreaming about him, an exquisite shuddering overwhelms her.' Is that what it is? 'She got wet like a bitch', another phrase, heard from the mouth of a man at a carnival or a party or a bar or perhaps Georges.

She tries again. Yes, the face leans down, the T-shirt with the wolf, and already it's tight like a fist between her thighs and there's that whooshing, she leans this man down towards her as far as she can, and all of her, body and head and brain and marrow and skull and bones, everything is alive.

She drops her bike in the grass, steps over the nettles. It's that time in summer, the slack time, deep in summer, when the days to come are as long as those that have gone.

Billie Jean is not my love.

The river is swollen with green water. Bulging, as if swifter water was surging beneath the surface. The soil is on delayed time, it remains there, dusty, shot through with this other matter, this other possible arrangement of matter. Without the slightest ripple, the whole expanse of water spreads over the muddy beaches. The softness of the silence is horrifying.

She lies down under the trees, it's the green from primary school, the green you imagine when you think of green. She could stay there forever, tumbling among the trees with her too-big body sore from bike-riding, sweating, hot—lying down to soothe this stabbing sensation that makes her rush outside, onto the roads, across the countryside, it's impossible to stay inside—remembering the incredible sequence of gestures and words that led her behind the pillar at Milord's—with this sun shining for no reason, when Rose and whoever are at the beach or lying around a pool, when towns are pulsating with their nightclubs, which are no doubt different from Milord's—when, on the disco ball, Paris and New York are pulsating and this village is the only dark spot—she dips her fingers in the water, slowly sinking her hands in up to the wrists.

The stupidity of this life, that she even needs this stupid body, the bother of it all. She dips her face in her cupped hands, it smells like cold rock and iron, the water runs between her breasts, their ridiculous shape. Her skirt drags and sticks to her thighs, and her pubis is outlined in an upside-down Y—this insistent presence, both empty and full, hungry and glutted—is she the only one to be so obsessed by it?

The adult world seems to worry about it a lot, and the whole school always has, but what connection is there between this raging loneliness that makes her stretch her legs restlessly in the cold water, and the piss 'n' shit of buttocks and unzipping pants and *whore-faggot-fuck-prick*, as if guys' underpants were opened by their mouth.

It's a ritual; her father brings back samples for her, a jar of Air Inter jam and a red, white and blue paper napkin, and this time a present in a little packet: a key ring. An Eiffel Tower that twinkles.

'There's something I need to tell you.'

Everything will be explained. The past, the present and the future. Their gestures, their words, everything that's incomprehensible. Just thinking about it makes her want to cry. (Solange is very sensitive.)

'There's this disease,' her father says to her. And he stops as if to tell himself what he's going to say. He's in his uniform, he smells like he always does, the smell of the air. And it's as if suddenly he's making it up, that he's making up the disease. 'It's a disease that kills people who begin with H. Homosexuals, Haïtians, Haemophiliacs and Heroin addicts.'

She doesn't know half of the words. Homosexual she knows, that means faggot. For girls you say dyke, but there aren't any here (except the hairdresser with cropped hair and the little chain around her ankle).

'The truth is that this disease is transmitted by fucking. And everyone fucks. Do you understand? So: fucking is forbidden.'

She's frightened he's going to start yelling. And forbid her, yelling at her.

'Do you hear me?'

Yes.

He lights a cigarette. He is very handsome. Very tall, his uniform trimmed with a badge in the shape of wings. Very short hair, grey at the temples, and a determined chin (says her mother).

'You believe me?'

Well, yeah.

'Don't be an idiot. Sharpen your critical faculties a bit. You really think I can forbid you from fucking? Only your mother believes stuff like that. Everyone fucks. I fuck, you fuck, we fuck.'

From his pocket he takes out a square, sealed packet, through which a round shape is visible. 'You know what this is, right?' He hands it to her. 'The first bastard who tells you this is useless, you send him over to me and I'll smash his head in. You make him put this on. You *make* him, do you hear me? If you catch this disease, it's death in two years. I've seen open graves. It's a bloodbath. You can only see them from the plane. And we have orders to close the blinds on the window seats. Do you know what that means? You go to the pharmacy, and she'll give you some. On my behalf. As many as you want.'

He takes the square packet out of her hand and tears the wrapping. He changes his mind and returns it to her.

It smells powerfully of rubber.

'You practise on a banana. And you *make* him, do you understand? It's forbidden to die. Understood?'

I went out with a fireman, she announces to Rose and Concepción.

She's not sure about saying that she slept with him. That would be too much of a lie. Okay, it's not written on your forehead. But she thinks it's obvious—with Rose it is. *Deflowered.* Like a bush that has been stripped of its flowers. There's a sort of reserve about Rose now. Perhaps she always had it. It's almost a matter of principle, with certain girls. If she had to draw up a list of them, it would include: Rose, Concepción, and perhaps Delphine, the girl from the chateau. Not Nathalie because she's a bit slutty.

For example, the same reserve or dignity found its full expression in Sixtine, on the beach three or four years ago, when she said she was 'indisposed'.

Rose. Now that she's done it, got rid of it (popped her cherry, the boys say), this thing that keeps her dignified and composed has spread out in her, like a great tree of honesty and pain, of honest pain, which has filled her up from top to bottom and made her a woman.

And she, Solange, is still just a floppy sack, *immature*, the head teacher wrote on her report. So it's obvious, it's obvious in the clear light of day. That she hasn't done it. That's what's so obvious.

Apparently in the vagina there's some thick skin that blocks the way through. That explains the butchering Rose suffered, and other stories she's heard, or read in *Girls Magazine*. Boys who were banging on it like it was a closed door, who ripped it to shreds. And then there are the roosters whose chopped-off heads are left to bleed on the bridal sheets of girls who are *not virgins* and who don't bleed. It's all too crazy. Like vampire stories.

'A bit of red ink would work just as well,' says Nathalie.

'Or get married when you've got your period,' Solange says.

Everyone laughs. She's surprised at her success—it was just elementary critical thinking.

'Other way round,' interrupts Nathalie. 'You have to calculate the dates so you're not on the rag. Because hanging round all day at the church while you're "indisposed" and all that, hello stress, as well as a red stain on the white dress. I'm telling you, it'd be so embarrassing.' Nathalie came back from a weekend in Bordeaux with 'hello stress' and 'I'm telling you'.

'It's so gross to be "indisposed" in church,' adds Rose, who is also trying out expressions, which suit her in the same way as her new haircut: bizarrely. (She has the same blond highlights as Sixtine. But on Rose, who is a brunette, they make her look like a zebra.)

'It ith forbidden to go into a church if you are indithpothed,' announces Concepción, whose embarrassment exaggerates her Spanish lisp—no one makes fun of her because now everyone starts to have their say. Even Christian.

Because he hangs out with the girls, Christian gets called a faggot: but *that's just it,* he likes girls—he says it with that earnest look people get when they're saying something important. It's so cool when Christian is there and they dare to talk about these things. And, except for Concepción, who gives up trying, the others all stare straight ahead and talk in voices like on the TV.

'I will never let my husband touch me when I'm "indisposed",' assures Rose, with that solemnity, that ice-queen halo she's acquired since she became a woman. Someone should take a Polaroid of her to capture what's taken hold of her—like seeing ghosts around haunted people.

If only they could get back to her fireman story. *I went out with a fireman.* Or *I went out with a fireman and everything happened so fast between us.* Or *He's experienced. And an exquisite shuddering*...If Christian could only know. The lips, the hands, the flashing lights. The big face leaning in. The fingers pushing in...Her legs folding and melting away, to carry her off limp and liquid...

Another girl, Slurp, interrupts them to ask for a light. Another big discussion follows (obviously there's not going to be any fireman). Until then she'd thought Slurp was called Slurp because she *sucks*. Sucks, sucks *what*—stay cool and think, it's not that difficult to imagine. It is certainly incredible but no more than *coupling*; 'it happens in the best families', even Christian agrees.

But the truth is more subtle, just like the truth is never exactly what you believe, the truth is complex and full of unexpected things, and the truth about Slurp is that when she was deflowered—by a member of the basketball team, the international team, one of those guys from Orthez, a hunk, really tall (so his dick was probably really big?)—he nearly got stuck.

Apparently the skin in Slurp's vagina was really thick, like leather. The international basketballer went at it with all his athletic powers, but nothing happened. He decided to put on a condom. It worked (thanks to the *lewdbrication* of the condoms). But when he pulled out, the condom stayed jammed in there, the vagina skin was like a plumber's seal. With a gynaecologist's flourish of his thumb and index finger, the international basketballer pulled and the condom spurted out with a slurp.

That's what surprises Solange most in the story: the attention to detail in the ending. She can imagine herself in the story, with her fireman. That could have happened to her. A close call.

And like a book that you understand better on reading it again when you're older (the wordplay in *Astérix*, or the sex scenes in Barjavel's novels) she now understands *slurp* better—the noise, not the girl. It teaches her about the fact that it's normal to be wet. And about how narrow young vaginas are: what the gynaecologist said wasn't just about her, which is on the whole reassuring, but still worrying—whatever, she knows what she's getting at. Anyway, wasn't the noise more likely to have been the squelching of blood?

In any case the whole operation seems difficult. Including the embarrassment of having a dumb idiot run around describing his exploits to everybody (because it's unlikely that Slurp herself would have spread the rumour); it all has nothing to do with her, it only happens to girls like Slurp.

She has to do it, but discreetly, with style, without going too far. She has to behave just like Sixtine did when she was 'indisposed' but was so casual about it. She practises having that expression, that slightly wounded attitude.

Since she found out about Slurp's story, it's like the river has been soiled by it. On the sandy banks of this pretty river, there are more and more condoms. The pretty river where she retreated with her sensitivity.

Her mother is in the kitchen, radio on, one Monday when the shop is shut, anyway, it's not about what the shop brings in. 'You should know,' she tells her (she wants to run away and block her ears), 'you should know that your mother was not destined to run a boutique, no, your mother had other projects in life, I had to sacrifice the things that were close to my heart, any old idiot can sell trinkets. Solange, first think about yourself, about what you want. What you really want. Before you get married, Solange. Before you get married.' Her mother always says 'boutique' for the shop, it's so annoying.

Her mother will probably go away for a few days. She needs some time to herself. 'Are you listening to me?'

Yes, she tries to be nice. It's not easy for her mother, it's never been easy for her mother. But she is back there, at Milord's, where lips are touching, where hands are grabbing. It's amazing, she can just call it up and the film runs—not the film—that moment, that time...life.

Hands. Lips. Finger. Her cunt is already hot, tight, wet, she just has to touch herself and she comes. 'Your father and I,' her mother is saying—and for the umpteenth time she wonders if her parents do it, this business of dick in fanny, but it seems too crazy, in this kitchen with Radio Monte-Carlo and the formica table sticky with jam. 'Your father and I'—her father's dick in her mother's fanny. Of course they did it for her, at least once (and for the other one, the boy in the photo). Unless she was adopted, but the similarity between her and her father is too striking (so they say).

The disco ball at Milord's. The fireman's dick blinking. What a fool she is not to have got his telephone number. Perhaps she's fallen in love? She wants to give herself to him. She could tell Rose: I fell in love and I gave myself to him. And tell Christian. He possessed her violently. And go looking for him far and wide, over hill and dale. Hopelessly.

All she has to do is ring the emergency number for a fire engine. Dial 18. Or go back to Milord's. And—it's a sign—the bass line of 'Billie Jean' starts up in the kitchen, drowning out her mother's voice. The memory is so violent—she's going to wake up at Milord's with the fireman's finger right there.

'I like this song,' her mother breaks off talking and taps her fingernails on the formica—Solange squeezes her legs together on the clammy *boum boum*.

She's a bit cold in her sequinned T-shirt, but the weather is mild, it's the speed that's making her shiver. The trees rush past, misty and full of screeches, the bushes are swaying and twisting, field mice, weasels and hedgehogs, the whole forest is alive. And she's supposed to stay locked inside. It's so pathetic.

On the incline she pedals hard, a few cars, flashes of headlights, sprays of gravel. It's very dark. Her father was meant to have repaired the dynamo for her bike light ages ago; she'd be better off asking Bihotz to do it. She rides on the path behind the public fountain to avoid running into people. It's bumpy. All she can hear is her bike, like chimes in the silence. She wonders if the Boursenave boy, the weird one, gets round at night like this. (In those situations, says

Nathalie, you just kick them in the balls. Don't hesitate, the window of opportunity is narrow.)

The industrial estate. Warehouses. Gym Tonic. The red sign of the Cheap Carpet outlet. Milord's is in sight, the car following can't make up its mind to pass her, she pedals in its headlights, surfing her huge dual shadow, two pedalling Solanges crossing and criss-crossing, the blinding white road, the pink and green neon lights, a corner—she accelerates, her shadow wheels spinning figures of eight and infinity signs, the car is still behind her, the noise of the motor completely drowning out the fields, a bullbar in her mudguard—she'd better stop, deal with it, can't see a thing, thank goodness she's not in a skirt, it passes her, a white Peugeot J7 van, and she hears:

'How far do you think you'll get with that?'

Shit. Bihotz.

Leave me alone, Monsieur Bihotz.

He looks like a madman.

Leave me alone!

But he snatches up her bike as if it's a toy and throws it, *bang*, in the back of the van. He grabs her bag. Her miniskirt and stick of mascara fall out.

LEAVEMEALONELEAVEMEALONEFUCKOFF!

Scruffy, ragged, like a giant smoking flare in the red of the van's warning lights, he lifts her up by an arm and throws her forward, an enormous fist, metallic, a mechanical digger. She's a little package, bendable and compactable.

'What am I going to say to your parents when we find you run over in the middle of the night, what am I going to say to them when you get yourself kidnapped by a lunatic?'

Her heart is banging inside her chest. To the green and pink rhythm of the Milord neon sign. Switching the screaming face on and off. She shows him her arm, where he has shaken her: *I'm the one who's going to say to my parents, take a look at that mark, there.*

He drives very fast. He doesn't head home. He goes straight ahead, the green and red lights disappearing behind them, the dreadful night closing in, and she's being carried off, not the slightest opening in the darkness.

She's in her tracksuit pants—the pants she put on ostensibly to wear to bed.

'Are they more practical for sneaking out? More practical for bike-riding? And that skirt up to your pussy, where do you slip into that—in the car park?'

He's completely ridiculous, there's no way she's going naked in Milord's car park, she already has her sequinned T-shirt on (she shows him), and she was going to put on the skirt first *then* take off her tracksuit pants underneath.

'Bloody hell!' He's shouting in a flat monotone. Sentences as long as the road. He's really sorry to have such sharp hearing and to have his antenna tuned to her every movement. He's upset about the number of sleeping pills her mother takes. He disapproves of her father's busy job. Her father must be flying to Paris now, isn't that right? He starts talking in that way she hates: as if he didn't need to breathe anymore, as if he had another body, another voice. 'You are so irresponsible!' he shouts.

She sees the tiny radius in which they move around, from the bottom of the village to Milord's, from the hill to the lake. Seen from up there, seen from an aeroplane, they are the only things moving on these sleepy roads.

'Fuck!' he shouts.

She's pretty sure he's going overboard with all this. Like the time he caught her watching the porn movie on TV. Just the thought of it. Even with the scrambled signal and the grey zigzagging images. The voices, the cries, over the buzzing of the broadcast. Just the thought of it.

Like I'm the first person in the whole world to sneak out.

Apparently Delphine, from the chateau, sneaks out (and you'd have to really want to, what with those spikes on all the railings).

He swears one day they'll find her in the cornfield with her throat slit. And what will he say to her parents? Her sweet little body. The ripped T-shirt, scattered sequins, traces of the struggle, and her whore's skirt hitched up to her belly. Her incredibly precious fifty kilos. Does she really have to get around like that, as if there was some connection, between her moving around on the Earth's crust, and... what in the end? What's the difference between that and the same thing that gets under Lulu's skin twice a year and makes her scratch at the fence and end up digging tunnels?

'What's the difference?' he yells.

He gets out of the J7 and stands in front of the black water, surveying the emptiness—and he smokes, just like her father, making the wisps of tobacco snap like her own small bones.

What if she got out really quietly and started running—but he's turning round already, What's the Time Mr Wolf? Statues, except that's all over, the games, having fun.

'What?' he asks like a thug, as if he was the one who was surprised, in the wrong, and furious.

The lake spreads out like an oil slick, hardly moving, a thick layer over the stupid little beach. She feels her chin puckering and her mouth twisting, the lake inhales her and liquefies her, she bursts into tears—such a defeat—*You won't say anything to my parents?* She argues her case, she wrestles with him. She grabs him, she pleads with him, she drenches him with her tears, she's on the verge of confessing to everything, including the fireman at Milord's, or of pretending that Rose and Nathalie are waiting for her, but he extricates himself and—?—he takes off his runners, his overalls and his T-shirt, and he enters the water: legs, buttocks, belly, arms, his big white body cuts through the surface like a pair of scissors, his head like a hairy button moves forward in the blackness, he swims.

Because you're allowed to do that, but not go to Milord's?

She could run away, but here he is coming back again, splashes of white on the fantastically black water, he powers towards her, his arms stirring up the night, a heavy, invisible substance, as he freestyles the emptiness.

And then he sits there, dripping in the seat, blowing his nose over the steering wheel. He's making bubbles like a crab. 'Sorry. Sorry.' She's the one who should be crying. He's shivering, sopping wet.

She'd like to say something, but no, she's not forgiving him, she doesn't see how she can forgive him for stopping her—right there on the road, and using force—from doing what she wants. And anyway, as if it had anything to do with forgiving, when he's just doing what a father would, or a brother if she had one, or even Terry or the fireman or any man really?

Monsieur Bihotz. It's okay. Stop. Stop it.

She puts her hand on his shoulder, clumsily. He leans over and lies down on her, grasping her hard by the hips, his heavy head buried in her thighs as he hiccups. Tiny little kisses sputtering on her wet tracksuit. Underneath she's wearing one of her mother's G-strings so she squirms: he mustn't see it or feel it, and the kisses are going all over her belly (what has he done with the bag that has her miniskirt in it?) and she can see quite clearly that his dick is doing that thing again, pointing at her, some supersized finger huge with reproach, whore's skirt, trollop. 'Little tart,' he said to her one day when she was at the public fountain with

Christian even though she wasn't doing anything wrong.

Is he asking forgiveness for that as well, for when he talks too much (but no more than her father or even her mother, if she thinks about it), for the mark on her arm (which has already disappeared), for the fright he gave her, for the stink of his sweat, his dick, his fat belly, or what exactly is he sorry for?—later on she'll work out the meaning of this apology—he squeezes her too hard, 'Solange, my Solange, my sunshine, my only angel,' sorry for that, for precisely what he's in the middle of saying, and sorry for squeezing her too hard, sorry for crying, sorry for saying sorry. She taps his head and murmurs sounds, *shhh, it's okay, come on, let's go*, if she could take the wheel, she would drive him home, *home, Monsieur Bihotz*.

He rings the doorbell, she's barely awake, he rings again and wants to see her mother and she's not going to let that happen, *If you have something to say to her you can just say it to me*, he pushes her aside, she moves ahead, she runs, *Coffee, Maman?*, she selects the beans one by one, use the ground coffee, darling, I've got a bad headache.

'Can you leave the room,' asks Monsieur Bihotz, it's more like a command—in her own home, you've got to be kidding. But her mother is at that point between sleeping tablets and her third coffee where even the thought of loud voices, of a fight—'I can't look after her anymore,' announces

Bihotz, he's going to spill the beans.

'Who?' Her mother looks surprised.

For a split second, she and Monsieur Bihotz are standing opposite this woman who seems to think that he's referring to the dog, Lulu. Then the triangle realigns itself. 'Solange'—her name spills out like a packet of flour.

'I can't do without you, Monsieur Bihotz!' Her mother screams the truth. He replies that he has to find a real job. 'Out of the question, Monsieur Bihotz, what with the financial crisis, especially around here.'

And Solange is watching out for the words that will determine the outcome, *sneak out, that night Solange, sequinned T-shirt and whore's skirt.* Oddly enough, there's a look of hesitation on Monsieur Bihotz's face, in his eyes and on his lips. He doesn't seem to believe what her mother is saying.

'Money shouldn't be a problem between us, Monsieur Bihotz'—'Perhaps she's old enough to look after herself'—'Old enough, out of the question'—'Solange, go to your room!'

She starts climbing the stairs and they unfold around her; she has this vision of herself climbing the stairs that are unfolding around her, and it keeps going, her hand on the banister, her body turning, her eyes looking at her hand on the banister; something is vibrating between her and the walls as if she no longer knows where her body belongs; she is here, from now on she will remain here, without being able to touch, feel, or be in any particular place—in this body that's like a lifejacket—she picks up a piece of Playmobil, places it in the palm of her hand, *click*, nothing happens, it lasts forever, the gesture, her hand, as if she was watching the film of herself watching herself.

She hears a voice begging, whispering, 'This child and me, all alone, you understand, Monsieur Bihotz.' She leans over the banister and sees a strange body, two shapeless heads, several arms, her mother leaning against Monsieur Bihotz, speaking into his navel, repeating 'my husband', sobbing, disgraceful, sloppy and spilling over—she should *sneak out* forever but she has to stay, she still has to stay here.

There's a party on at the chateau, up there, at Delphine's. Next Saturday. She's not invited. Of course she's not invited. She hardly knows Delphine. But Rose is, invited, and even the cousins, Sixtine and Meredith (not Alma, who is doing a Baroque singing internship somewhere in the Ardèche).

Her suffering is almost unbearable. By herself in her bedroom, she falls to bits. Without people looking at her, without a witness to her existence, her atoms abandon her. Dust motes floating to the window panes, a fine cloud, a veil punctured by beams of light.

Riding her bike along the river, she sees the chateau up there, suspended in the air, like a transfer or a sticker. As if it wasn't real. She can't even bear dogs anymore. The way Lulu jumps up on her as soon as she arrives; whereas she

(Solange) doesn't know what to do with herself anymore, go into the house, not go in, eat, not eat, go out, sleep, die.

The Tour de France and Bihotz in front of his TV.

'What's the matter?' Bihotz asks. 'What's wrong with you?'

She's started calling him Bihotz and it drives him mad.

'Delphine? The Peyreborde girl, from up there? She'll call you. She's just forgotten. My mother did the cleaning there, at the chateau, and she used to take you with her. You used to say there were ghosts there. During August they had white sheets draped over all the armchairs.'

So she's compelled to reminisce along with him, and the memories come back. And she talks to him and he makes her feel better, this hick, this *metalhead* who listens to Iron Maiden.

The white shapes, the windows open onto a sky of dense, leafy green trees, the colour and the slant of those hazy days. There was a swimming pool. She was absolutely forbidden to go near it.

She's sharing all this with him and it's so annoying. This guy who has nothing to do with any of it. This *anomaly* (these days she's learning new words).

'But the Peyreborde girl is not from the chateau,' he says. 'The d'Urbide family lives in the chateau. The Peyreborde family lives in the concierge's lodge.'

He's carrying on as if he knows her girlfriends better than she does. And probably her whole life while he's at it. (No, no one will ever understand her, not the real her.)

'But what's the matter with you?' wails Bihotz. 'You weren't like this before. You don't have to act all grown up. No one's looking at us.'

It infuriates her how he makes a scene about everything, while she just deals with it. When she remembers how Nathalie told her that Rose thought that she (Solange) was *perverse*, supposedly because she was worried about her, but how happy she (Rose) must have been showing off with *perverse*! (She looked it up in the dictionary, it means almost neurotic. *Perverse*, what a joke. Rose has just got a really big head, that's all, she's so full of herself, she uses those words to make herself seem interesting, like she's the centre of the world.)

'Are you listening to me?' says Bihotz. 'You're like the girl in *The Exorcist.* Are you going to start speaking backwards or what?'

Nathalie says that if you listen to Iron Maiden backwards, you hear messages from the Devil.

'Call Delphine. Invite her to afternoon tea. It's a misunderstanding. A complete misunderstanding. Do you want me to call her? I know her mother.'

When he was little, Monsieur d'Urbide smacked him because he was picking plums in the garden, plums that were on the ground, plums from the chateau, with Delphine's mother…

That's the forty-eighth time you've told me that, change the record.

He picks up the phone and he does it: he calls the chateau.

Delphine is coming for afternoon tea. That bitch who is having a party and not inviting her. She chooses the music carefully. Jimi Hendrix, that's cool; no one knows it, but she listened to it with him when she was little, so she arranges for Delphine's knock at the window to occur at exactly the same time as a guitar riff, a riff that shocks fat Delphine.

And from four until six, they finally talk properly. Obviously there's the old reflex of showing off, so there's a fair amount of crap in their chat, but at six o'clock Delphine has to leave and there's been no mention of the party.

If she mentioned it first, that would ruin everything, she understands that now: the need to respect social convention in order to respect yourself, even if Delphine is not the sort of girl you'd respect, she's not at all *a popular girl*, whatever, she knows what she's getting at. Anyway, you have to have a lot of experiences like this, have afternoon tea with lots of really different girls, you learn what people are like, you shape your identity in relation to them; that is, you learn who you are. It's really creepy how Rose and Nathalie are so narrow-minded, it's racism, pure and simple. They should open their eyes and look around: there are miserable people everywhere!

Still, you're allowed to have parties, aren't you?

'No,' says Delphine. 'My mother is a real bitch.'

But the party this Saturday?

'No, it's the landlady's daughter who's having the party. They're the only parties my mother lets me go to. It's an act of *charity* from the d'Urbide girl. Just like my clothes: she gives me her old stuff. But she's thinner than I am.'

So you don't live in the chateau?

'Yes, I do, in front of it.'

In front?

'The place at the front is the concierge's lodge.'

Oh my God, you are such a liar!

'I do live at the chateau, just in front of it.'

All those years you carried on like you were the princess of the chateau.

Delphine denies it, says she's never pretended that.

But you let people think that.

'If people believed it, that's their problem.'

Right from kindergarten.

'Yeah, like when Bidegarraï said a parachutist had landed on the roof of his house. Same thing. We were kids.'

In her mind's eye, she had always pictured that parachutist on the Bidegarraï house, as clearly as the church tower in the village square (there never was a parachutist?). So what, back to the party business. She should offer to go with Delphine as if it was an act of *charity*, to this loser girl, so weirdly dressed, so *concierge* ('to the council holiday camp, with the kids of concierges?' Sixtine had exclaimed when Rose went there). But Delphine seems strangely self-assured and gives her a look of defiance (or pity?):

'Shit, Solange, do you really think there are people who still believe your father's a pilot?'

Her face catches fire.

'Your father is a *porter*. Do you think I didn't know? Rose saw him carrying her bag when she went to England.'

Suddenly there is no more oxygen in the room. Pretend nothing has happened. Pretend to be what she has always been: the daughter of an Air Inter pilot and a shopkeeper from Clèves-le-Haut.

The girl who's having the party is called Lætitia, Lætitia d'Urbide; that means *Happiness* in Latin. There are at least fifty people, even high school kids and guys from the coast, and punch in salad bowls with ladles.

Stand up straight, like an air hostess.

Rose doesn't seem surprised to see her. Nor embarrassed, or anything. Perhaps she's already drunk a fair bit. But it's impossible to have any contact with Rose now. To get anywhere near her, to be in the same space as her. It's as if a river separated them: Rose and her Parisian cousins and Lætitia d'Urbide on one bank, she and Delphine on the other bank. The same bank as Peggy Salami. With the weirdos, the hicks, the concierges, the badly dressed, the *perverse*, the squalid, those with big chins, the families with ten kids, the outliers, the people who've had the same car forever and a yard full of tyres. Like at the Bihotz place.

To be labelled a Bihotz.

She serves herself a ladle of punch, drinks it in one go and starts to sway her hips. *Let's Dance*. She knows the lyrics by heart; she learned them off the record sleeve, at Rose's, as it happens. 'That girl is gifted,' Rose's mother had said.

She will never go to Rose's again. Never again.

Rose's father is a teacher and her mother is a sort of assistant art teacher. Sure, they don't live in a chateau but their house is definitely cool and so, what's the word, welcoming.

She wants to cry.

Let's Dance.

Her skirt is falling down, it's so awkward. First she had put on her shiny gym leggings, and thrown together a very short skirt and a white jersey hooded top, with just a narrow band showing under her V-neck pullover, which she'd worn back to front, and a fake leather belt that sits perfectly on her hips, very Madonna, and some pink spray in her hair and her fake Dockside shoes. And then she took the whole thing off (just as well she'd got started early); she borrowed her mother's Prince of Wales check skirt, her father's black Polo shirt, and it ends up being a really fantastic outfit that looks neat, *New Wave*, with her imitation Docksides and big white clips in her hair to liven up the effect, and black mascara, and she's teased her hair to give it lots of volume. But in no time it's all hanging flat again. And the skirt is slipping.

She bought some Kool menthol cigarettes and managed

to get hold of some Get 27 liqueur; they go well together. Perhaps she shouldn't have drunk it on top of the punch because she's starting to freak out. Which is bad when you want to have a good time at a party and go really crazy.

She heads to the toilet so she can hitch the skirt up a bit higher. She is too fat. She makes a solemn resolution, on the spot, to replace a meal a day with cigarettes.

The d'Urbide parents don't seem to be at the chateau. They *really* are called d'Urbide, with an apostrophe—'fucking toffs,' says Delphine, who is disgustingly vulgar, a real fishwife. The only adult in the vicinity is Delphine's mother, who hangs round the whole time, cleaning up glasses. Right now, in fact, she is wiping the floor. Can Delphine do anything she wants in front of her *fucking bitch* of a mother? It must be difficult. Like when Rose's father was Rose's teacher.

She says hello to Delphine's mother so as not to appear a snob. Someone has put on Sade, the soft voice that envelops everything; it's nice and some of the bad vibe of the evening dissipates.

'I feel pretty shit,' says Delphine, who has turned red, and looks fatter than Solange has ever noticed. 'Do you want to go for a walk?'

Right now I'm dancing.

'Come on, my boyfriend gave me some dope.'

This is the moment to absorb the fact that Delphine *smokes*, and that she has a *boyfriend*. The moment to observe Delphine rolling a *joint*. On the terrace opposite the rose garden and the tennis courts. Under the dazzling white moon. Using a cassette case to mix and cut the tobacco.

You're so introverted. But we had a good talk last time, didn't we. I told you everything. (That she was going out with a fireman.)

Delphine seems bored. 'Food and sex are two things that shouldn't exist,' she declares.

Right, so she's already done it. The concierge's daughter smokes and has already done it.

'What do you think I've got to look forward to?' Delphine asks her, passing her the joint.

What should she say? Is it a real question, like in a horoscope? Or just a statement: nothing? She takes a drag and it's good, better than her Kools, and the effect is a bit stronger.

'Like even you,' Delphine continues, 'you'll have more than I will. You can tell straight away. The proof is, like, you don't even know what I mean.'

And from this perspective, in the evening light, in front of this fabulous garden, Delphine is almost beautiful, deep, unusual (if you ignore the 'like even you' and the 'like, you don't even', in fact if you ignore what comes out of her mouth).

Christian and Rose are kissing on a couch. It's disgusting. Being jealous would be really humiliating. A total waste of time, for a feeling *that is just not worth it*, that is completely degrading.

Look nonchalant. Like an air hostess.

A degrading feeling, quite simply *degrading*.

Lætitia is kissing a guy too. She's wearing a dress. The girl's wearing a dress. Full and flowing, with a belt made of big gold chains. She (Solange) would look like a grandmother if she wore it, but Lætitia looks amazingly hot in it. So weird. Her legs are as thin as her arms, and she's wearing opaque stockings, they're perfect, and the guy's arm is going up and down them. You can't tell if his hand is at the top, at the bottom, in front, behind, it's winding around, it's grazing the bare part of her thigh. The music (someone has put Sade back on) is coming out of those fingers playing on those stockings. *Stockings*, the girl's wearing stockings, which are staying up by themselves, a black band on a white thigh under a black dress, appearing, disappearing, white, black, thigh, dress, the hand moves onto the band of lace, the girl gets up followed by the guy with his wandering fingers and wild eyes, they disappear into the rolling shadows.

'They're going to fuck,' someone says in her ear. A guy who drags on a joint and passes it to her. 'Every party she goes upstairs with someone. There are *so many* bedrooms up there.'

He's older than her. More like Year Ten or Eleven. Black eyelashes and green eyes. She takes a drag of the joint and steps back a bit (nonchalantly). The glow of the dress is still floating in the shadows, the flash of the chains on the big belt, the hand of the suitor tracing curves and crowning her, Lætitia, the happy one, the princess upstairs who devours them all with kisses.

'Do you know what they call her?'

Lætitia d'Urbide?

'Yeah…' He inhales deeply on the joint and holds his breath, like you're supposed to.

I don't know. Læti?

He laughs. He laughs with his mouth open, without a sound, for a long time. As if she's said something cute. 'Cheap Carpet.' He expels it with the smoke. It's like there's a shifting meaning in what he's saying: not so much the nickname, which is striking, as the inventiveness of the village kids, these hicks with such funny ways of behaving.

She can see the carpet outlet next to Milord's. She wants to be back there. Under the flashing light. No. Actually, no. She wants to be where she is. With the guy collapsed on this couch.

Why Cheap Carpet?

The boy lets out a groan which is in fact a concentrated laugh, the sort of laugh that would emerge if he became detached from his body (she imagines, surprised by her own thought process).

Then she has the revolting thought that you can get it on the cheap with Lætitia. Cheap Læti. Or that the boys are using her as a doormat. As carpet. Lying on her, walking on her, crushing her, delousing themselves on her like monkeys.

'She's got hairs on her breasts,' says the boy. 'Cheap Carpet does.' His mouth open in silent laughter, as if he was holding up the nickname like a museum relic, a scalp or something.

She pictures her own breasts. She had never thought about this problem—no, phew, she does not have hairy breasts. At least she's avoided this defect. She laughs.

He takes the joint back from her and their fingers touch.

'Where are you from?'

Time is behaving strangely. It speeds up and then slows down. Lætitia and the guy have just left the room, but she (Solange) has had time (eternity or fixed time) to have more thoughts than during her whole life so far, time to think that she has thought more things.

From the coast.

'That's weird, I've never seen you there. What's your name?' He passes the joint back to her, moistened with his saliva.

She is about to say Charlotte. Or Sandra. Or Jennifer.

Solange. What's yours?

His name is Arnaud. He's from the coast too.

Time loops again. Or pauses. Or *rewinds. Let's Dance*, that song again.

'I'm right into those freaky states where your mind is either really sharp, or completely spacey…' says the boy. 'I don't know which I prefer,' he continues, squashed up against her. 'A sharp mind is cool because all your senses are on total alert. But it kills you, it's so tiring. When you're high, a bit sleepy, it's good too, and you kind of experience things differently, I don't know, that's always when I'm able to really see things, problems, political problems, you totally understand them because you see the big picture, like from above, like the perspective aliens would have, you're outside everything and totally calm, as if nothing affected you; like a meeting of the student council but you wouldn't be at high school anymore, you would have passed your final year ages ago and you would understand everything, all the ins and outs. It diffuses everything, absolutely everything. It diffuses problems. And it's more interesting than alcohol. And you feel a lot less alone.'

I feel alone, too.

'At your age it's normal. I used to be such an egomaniac, I was less mellow than I am now. Because you can only define yourself in relation to others. In the beginning you have no consciousness, so no defined character, nothing about you is determined. Sartre said that. When you think about it, it's pretty amazing, totally amazing…'

That means that when I was tormenting myself, worrying who I was (she begins, surprised to know that she was tormenting herself), *and believing that I alone knew who I was, I mean alone in my head, in fact that was all stupid…*

'You can only define yourself in relation to others. That's the bottom line. Sartre said it. It's a fundamentally political thing.'

It's natural. It's the instinctive approach.

'I don't believe in instinct at all. What do your parents do?'

They died in an aeroplane crash.

'Listen, just be yourself. That's the best thing. Be yourself, in relation to others. Actually, it's your best *bet* anyhow, even in relation to others. We're always making choices, whatever happens. You can always choose, you are completely free. Everything that happens involves choices.'

I'd like to go to the USA. The Clèves Rotary Club is offering a one-year scholarship, all expenses paid, except the price of the trip. I've given it some serious thought. But right now I'm in a daze. I'm off my face. We always react in the same way to particular situations, don't we? I mean each one of us does. It's natural, right? Freedom is so fantastic.

'Actually it can backfire. Like, you always need an audience when you put on your own show, but needing an audience is not just for show, it's *real.* Otherwise you get crushed by despair. Someone, Hegel, said that there are two parameters in consciousness: time—chronology—and space—got it? space—and twelve squares, twelve categories in which you can put ideas, and that's how we gain access to knowledge.'

That really doesn't suit me (she argues, her head full of arcs and squares). *That's old school. It's too restrictive. For me the mind is completely limitless.*

'No way. The mind has limitations. But you have to

learn to use it one hundred per cent. It's fantastic. When you think about it. That means that telepathy...I mean, if we used our minds one hundred per cent, we could even speak to each other without words. Total comprehension. From one to one. It'd be perfect. We are awfully limited. Awfully limited. It's awful.'

Perhaps that's true, but it's probably false. How is it limited?

'Well, for example, right now, you think you're talking to me, but perhaps you're not. Perhaps you imagine that you're talking to me, but in reality I'm not listening to you. Whereas we could be talking directly, one to one. You see, it's better to experience the other, even if it makes you miserable, than to stay in your own personal safety zone. The main thing is to have flaws. Not just a clean and cosy little conscience.'

Definitely.

'Most people are drama queens, egomaniacs, but you just have to get through that stage and in the end it teaches you a good lesson. When people tell you, "Stop being a fuckwit," you might feel worse, but it does you good. In the long run. My father said it to me, stop being a fuckwit, and it was the best thing he could have done for me. Because all of a sudden you feel like an idiot. A few slaps—to say, "get over it, you don't have any real problems"—it does you good. Even if you don't have any parents, like you.' (She'd forgotten her parents were *dead*.)

'You can never go back to what you were before. You

can't regret experiences. You want to stay yourself, sure, but you can't go backwards. An experience is an experience. For good. You can't forget that you have learned things, not so much what you have learned but the very fact that you have learned. A girl like Cheap Carpet knows nothing about otherness...You can't go back to square one. Forget your little ego and face up to life, well, you know what I mean. You can't *dis-evolve*. Really.'

She has never spoken so well with anyone.

They climb a staircase with landings the size of whole rooms, the size of her bedroom (her two bedrooms: the one at her house and the one at Bihotz's house) (she's like a kid with divorced parents) (it's absolutely the first time she's thought that).

'You have an amazing arse,' the boy whispers into her neck.

Her skirt is slipping, it's so awkward.

She'd like to take back the stuff about her parents being dead because it's another huge lie and, as well as that, one day she'll have to introduce this boy to them (her parents) (and even to Bihotz) (no, not to Bihotz).

Up a step, another step, she pretends to trip, he holds her, he holds on to her, she gives a little gasp, drawing air in between her teeth, like Marilyn.

'Did you see that?'

On the landing there's an enormous painting with orange, yellow and red stripes that don't represent anything but look good.

'Her father owns all the vineyards north of here,' says the boy with a big sweep of his arm that includes the entire geographical world. 'He spends his whole life buying paintings, in the United States and everywhere, and the rest of the time he smokes in his smoking room and drinks.'

An old man passes them on the landing. A king.

Wow, she says.

The Earth is spinning on the end of Arnaud's hand. The staircase continues upwards.

And Lætitia is coming down, alone. Her lover is right now lying in a *pool of blood.* A little clinking of her gold chain belt. She's smoking, with an expression of disdain, her eyelids half-closed, her long legs set in slow motion in front of her, her patent-leather Doc Martens preceding her down the stairs step by step, as if the exertion has finally convinced her of the vanity of this world.

And, stock-still on the staircase, he's looking at her.

But she's the one he kisses. Solange. He hiccups as he squeezes her. He sticks his tongue in her mouth.

There's a huge stained-glass window on the final landing, a seascape lit by the moon, with the real garden, under maritime pines, visible behind it, in shades of blue, as if Clèves was turning into the sea, and the whole world was immersed in a marvellous connectedness.

The door they're leaning on opens behind them. They fall into a bedroom, laughing, their bodies entwined, he's holding her, he pushes her head down. He's pushing really hard, he's struggling with his fly and her head, to unzip and to hold her, time is doing one of its shadowy loops again, there's some rubbing of fabric and skin and then everything becomes clear: his dick is in her mouth. From the pumping action he's doing with her, she understands that she has to raise and lower her head. It's a bit lumpy down there, it smells bad and it tastes acidic.

He groans. Is she hurting him? She relaxes her jaw.

'Suck, for fuck's sake.' He sounds distressed.

She clamps her jaw again and tries to cope with putting pressure on his dick, as well as suction, a vacuum, that seems to be what he wants, like when you suck your thumb but bigger.

The taste has gone. There's a lot of saliva and a bit of it is running down her chin, tickling her, like the pubic hairs sticking up her nose. She's got used to the smell, but it's kind of a pity that she feels as if she's cleaning his dick. She'd like him to let go of her hair, it's hurting, and her arm is stuck in some kind of judo position. She's starting to get a sore jaw. The muscles on the side of her mouth are cramping up. Clearly she doesn't use them enough, in any case not like this. It must be a matter of practice. This business does seem to require opening your mouth a lot. She tries to think about other things, like when she's at the dentist.

'Fuck!' she hears, all of a sudden. 'I've ended up with a robot!'

She twists her neck to look at him. Her jaw relaxes and the skin on her skull slides back into place.

'You've really got zero imagination, haven't you? Do you actually have to be reminded to lick the penis from time to time? Run your tongue around it a bit, whatever!'

He mimes it, sticks his tongue out, stretches his neck. He looks weird, like he's in agony. A look she's already seen on Bihotz, the day he was holding his dick in his hand (or the day of the cup and ball game).

He shows her how to hold the base, her hand around it, not too hard, and every now and again to have a go at his balls underneath. He falls back on the bed, holds on to her hair and seems to feel better now.

She's got to play the part of the desirable girl, the one who knows what she's doing. *An exquisite shuddering.*

That's exactly what's happening right now. Right now she is doing that to a boy. The world is alive and she is at the centre of it.

But it takes so long. She tries thinking about the river running through the bottom of the garden. About the swimming pool at night (she can hear shouts, dives, laughter. She'll go down there later). The dick is driving into her brain. Ramming the back of her skull. It really is a pretty weird situation to be in. It's difficult to think about anything else. The cramp becomes unbearable, she tries to extricate herself and he screams: 'No! No way! No way!'

He gets up, with the thing at that strange angle and really stiff like she's seen on Bihotz. A spur. A bottle opener. He's intimidating, not so much his dick, but his angry pride. But it's true: she's behaving like a fool.

He starts from scratch again (in a daze but with precision): she's on her knees in front of him *pumping* him, he's grabbing on to her ears, his fingers digging into the back of her skull, he's slamming into her gullet and she wants to vomit, she coughs, she weeps, he yanks and pulls her, she coughs, her head is a coconut, a rattling money-box, there's nothing inside there and he cries out and something *revolting* fills her mouth.

She runs to the bathroom and spits. Rinses her mouth and breathes. In the mirror she looks awful. She fixes her hair with her fingers and tries to make her cheeks and eyelids less puffy with splashes of cold water. Her mascara has run and looks terrible. She rubs at it with the tip of her finger but that makes it worse. And the taste is still there. Something from outer space (as Bihotz would say). Slimy, sickly sweet, pervasive, appalling.

He's lying on the bed, eyes closed. 'You're a pretty inhibited girl,' he says, with a hint of tenderness. His dick is lying in a little grey pile outside his jeans.

'I mean, that could be kind of offensive for a guy. If you rush off to the bathroom and all that. It's gratifying for men when girls swallow. It's a nice way to finish the thing off...'

He opens his arms for her and kisses her on her hair.

'Dope slows me down. And with the alcohol on top of that...But that's why it'll be good for you later. We'll have plenty of time.' His dick lifts up slightly, it's crazy, all by itself, like the head of a lizard.

She's finding it hard to believe that she's here, for real, lying against a boy's chest, in the hollow of his shoulder. Not the usual make-believe, not the pillow on her little bed, no, a man, a real one.

He kisses her, on the hair again. Fair enough, what with that taste in her mouth. She'd like to brush her teeth. She must have bad breath. It'd be good if they could start talking again. She can't feel the effect of the dope anymore. He must think she's stupid. He's smoking a cigarette, his eyes on the light fitting. He looks brooding and mysterious. She doesn't know what to say.

The plaster mouldings on the ceiling. The wallpaper that has the same bird pattern as the Bihotz teacups, but with a more old-fashioned, *pastel* look. A Chinese screen and claw-foot furniture. The window opens onto a small terrace.

If only she could be Lætitia d'Urbide, a bit older. And stay with him in the chateau. They would have horses down by the river, tennis matches with guests. They would *disappear* together and he would *possess* her, and she would put her dress back on, he would tie the ribbons, perhaps tightening her corset, his knee pressed into her waist like she saw in a film, one last kiss in her unfastened hair, followed by a long embrace at the top of the stairs, she's leaning back, he's so proud of her, the master of her heart and soul, and he would marry her, the most beautiful girl of all, beaming in front of the swooning guests.

He stands up to get dressed and she realises in horror that she was rubbing herself against his thigh. But he starts telling her something: 'I was right up the front, pogo-dancing, I could touch the stage, there were girls fainting everywhere, it was totally crazy. We were so squashed that we didn't even realise the girls had fainted and were still standing up, can you believe it? The crowd was holding them up and it was like they were dancing and we were passing them over our heads to the roadies and then there was even a disabled guy in his wheelchair being handed over our heads, it was so cool of them to do it.'

She has the same taste as him in music, exactly the same. She must go to the Cure concert in Bordeaux. But she'd better get with it, that's precisely what he's talking about—the concert was last week.

'You've read the lyrics of Robert Smith's songs, haven't you? I mean you've *read* them? That combination of cynicism and edgy sensitivity. He really *feels* things. You don't realise unless you've read his lyrics, but it's even more complex than that: he's hiding his own feelings otherwise it's too painful. Cynicism is polite despair, it's cool, and it's totally the essence of Robert Smith.'

She doesn't dare mention Michael Jackson. Is Michael Jackson actually that cool after all? She'd really like him to go and get her something to drink, something strong, but would that be going too far?

He's rolling another joint.

Arnaud. *Arnaud.* She sighs as she whispers the 'r'.

'You look sort of wistful.'

He undoes the buttons on her Polo shirt, one by one.

She tries to look *wistful*, it's cute the way he said that.

'I hope you understand that none of this commits us to anything.'

Of course. Absolutely. She's so cool, open-minded.

'I wouldn't want you to suffer.'

He says it as if they were in a soap opera, and she realises that it's funny and that they are in this together. He takes off her Polo shirt, her father's Lacoste Polo (fortunately there are no stains on it or she'd be shot).

He kisses her on the neck and grabs her breasts. She hopes they're big enough, *big enough to fill the hands of an honest man.* She tries to pull him closer to her so he can kiss her neck again and pummel her breasts less. She breathes in deeply and then there's some kind of misunderstanding and he pushes on her head, holds her down, under the sea, under water. She can feel her tears welling like a huge wave of *cynicism*, the dick is cold and sticky, soft and full of wrinkles, he moves his abdomen impatiently and she gets going, she chews a bit (like the fatty bits on the chicken) and it expands, it really is a pretty wacky thing, it fills her mouth like an inflating balloon.

Tenderly, he tells her she's a little doggy. The word immediately sticks itself between her legs and she starts to get wet. Perhaps he's saying it in his sort of off-hand way, projecting the word from his mouth—in any case it sticks there like a muzzle.

'You've got potential,' Arnaud says, puffing. 'You're improving every minute. Stop, you'll make me *come*.'

And he turns her over, repositioning her with assurance, an assurance that lets a bounding puppy-dog loose in her underpants, until it hits her, and there's no doubt about it—he wants to do it. He lifts up her mother's Prince of Wales check skirt and sticks his dick in there.

She doesn't want to. Not like that. Not *back to front*. She wants to see his face, talk to him, see him. She struggles, she's drowning, she's in free fall.

He turns her back the right way. He takes her in his arms and strokes her hair. Says it's okay, that he's not going to rape her. He guides her hand to his dick and, with his hand over her hand, he sets up a sliding rhythm.

'It's okay if you're a virgin. You don't have to pretend. I'm the one who popped d'Urbide's cherry, and I have to say she really got off on it. She came, all right.' He takes a deep breath. 'On the other hand'—he relights the joint on the bedside table—'there are plenty of ways to stay a virgin, if that's what's bothering you.'

He shoves his hand into her hair. She applies herself to the pumping, now that she knows how to do it. She's got the rhythm, come on, I'll get you going, her skirt pushed up to her waist, his hand whacking at her bare breasts and sliding down between her legs where it's so wet now, little doggy, inflamed by the words, she keeps pumping, she pictures herself doing it, she sees both of them in this bedroom, her soggy underpants jammed between her buttocks, her twisted mouth and sweaty face slapped up against pubic hair and balls, back and forth, she's pumping him well. She'd like him to move his hand further down but it's annoying that either his arm is too short or she's too far away or something's stuck and yet it seems possible, she imagines, she has the feeling that all he'd have to do is to *finger* her and then she'd—'Ahh, you fat fucking bitch!'—the 'itch' bursts out of him in a piercing trill and she leaps away and the stuff spurts in the air and falls on her mother's skirt—shit.

She's not really *fat*. There are plenty of people fatter than her, like Delphine or even Rose, and anyway he is too—he's a bit like Bihotz in the belly department. Or was he saying it as a joke?

'That wasn't very nice of you,' he announces. He takes a drag of the joint, crushes the butt on the lampshade base and disappears into the bathroom.

She pulls the sheet back over herself and tries to rub out the burn mark on the lamp with some spit on her thumb. She listens to him having a long piss. The intimacy of gurgling urine. She fantasises again about the young bridegroom who, after sealing the secret pact, descends the staircase and casually greets the guests. His whole life in front of him to lie with her and lie with her again, while also looking after his horses, and coming up to find her again tomorrow and the day after and forever. She's only got a few seconds to rub herself, the flesh of her fingers on the flesh of her cunt, in a swift circular motion she is both the lord and lady at the same time and she pushes right inside her cunt, her belly flat on the bed, her thighs quivering, she *comes* in one huge surge.

Arnaud. She pretends to be asleep. She hears him going downstairs.

In the bathroom she examines herself in profile. How can she serve him up these fried eggs; he must know plenty of other better ones, and her areolas are ugly. Cheap Carpet's are much more attractive, even Delphine's are bigger. You probably have to *go all the way* before they grow.

She's not sure whether to go home to her place or to Bihotz's. Where will she have fewer questions to deal with? But when she gave her telephone number to Arnaud she got confused (the dead parents), and gave him Bihotz's number (*my tutor*) to memorise (Arnaud didn't have a pencil).

'What time did you go to bed?' Bihotz asks. He looks deep into her eyes as if a tunnel led right inside her, from the eye sockets to her *vagina* where her *cherry* is still in place.

One-fifteen.

Like those shutters that can block the viewfinder on telescopes.

'How's Delphine's mother?'

Yeah, she's good.

'So you saw that she's not the girl who lives in the chateau?'

Yeah, I got that.

He stops and she can finally get back to the movie in her head. Arnaud. His sly look. A pact. A silent agreement. Arnaud. The way he said it: *Stop, you'll make me come.*

She'd happily go to bed now but Bihotz will think that's odd, for a girl who went to sleep early last night. So she stays there, watching 'Stade 2' on TV, while he fondles Lulu.

You've got potential. 'Potential', that's in the future, which means he wants to see her again. And the way he moved, the firm grasp of his hand, a bit too firm but so much the *man in control.* Her breathing is getting shorter and she's wet between her legs. A future as a *courtesan.* Lounging under chandeliers and tapestries.

Carl Lewis is on his mark for the hundred metres. Carl Lewis runs so fast that it's already finished. Bihotz says the white guys will never have a chance. (But ever since she made up her mind about all that—the planet spinning pointlessly in empty space—politics does not interest her.)

She looks at the telephone as if it's a completely new object, a gateway, an antechamber to another world, with wall hangings and Chinese screens. She tries to remember if its ring is a 'dring' or a 'bli bli'. 'Bli bli' is the phone at her house, the new touch-tone telephone. She tries to hypnotise this one, the rotary-dial phone.

Dring.

She leaps up. She's Carl Lewis.

It's her mother. Asking if she's eating here or over there. No, no one has phoned. Was she expecting a call from Rose? From Nathalie? How was Delphine's?

23 57 01.

That's his number. She knows it by heart, it was imprinted in her memory straight away. 23 57 01. Two and three (the two of us and then a child?), five to seven like the secret rendezvous time, and zero and one (why zero and one?). Anyway if you add it all up, 2+3+5+7+0+1, it makes 18, adulthood, when she'll be free. Perhaps 18 is his age? There are so many things for them to discover about each other.

23 57 01.

Bihotz is going to lock up the chickens.

She lifts up the receiver and punches the numbers into the air. How are you? Very well and you. I was just thinking about you. I couldn't call you. Because. I was thinking about your mouth and your breasts. Yes, I mean it, they're amazing. You're so beautiful. No other girl has ever made me stiff like you do. You've got potential. Stop, you'll make me come. No other girl. You're more beautiful than. Stop, you'll make me come. I love you. Do you love me. I love you. Yes. Yes.

Bihotz comes back from the chickens.

Night falls.

Dring!

She picks up, her heart pounding terribly, she really is way too *cynical*—once again, it's her mother. Who is expecting her for dinner. Who has not seen her the whole weekend. I only have one daughter and I don't even see her. No, I told you to come and have dinner. I really wonder sometimes which way your head's screwed on. Do I really have to *ask* you to come and see me? What will it be like in a few years' time?

She spends the evening watching *2001: A Space Odyssey* with her mother.

She plays back the moment when he had his expert fingers in her and she felt like she was going to drown. *You look sort of wistful.* She's got to stop running her own movies in her head. She is a total *egomaniac.* Why would this straight-up *high school* guy call her at all? He's probably forgotten her number. As if he didn't have a pencil—so stupid.

There should be telephones with extendable cords that follow you wherever you go. Or actually without cords at all. Not that she has much to do, or places to go. Or even wants to.

'I don't recognise you,' says Bihotz. 'You used to be like a bee in a bonnet. Now you stay inside all the time, you look like Dracula. Come and help me with the corn.'

She feigns a headache.

'What the hell? Don't try the line about migraine.'

After two days of imprisonment, she really does have a headache. Her mother wants her to go to the doctor. She sounds so unbearably sympathetic.

A telephone cord to follow her bike, run along the roads after her, circle the village and come back here, a ball of twine winding tighter and tighter around her.

Bihotz puts on a shocking record, a slow dance song by the Scorpions: *I'm still loving YIIIOUOUOU* and his long hair sways as he shakes his head. 'You can put on your own records if you don't like it.'

23 57 01

Where should she be? Where should she go? Should she call him or not? What should she do? If only it would all stop. If only something would stop, so she didn't have to think about it anymore. So she could move on. One month later, one year later, two years later, three years later. And be sixteen. Eighteen. Such an unbearable wait. To be an adult. To be whatever it means to be a woman. To know how life works, what direction her life will take, who she will be. Be able to come and go, make phone calls, speak, go away. Fuck. *Fuck.* Take hold of the entire Earth and fuck.

She pictures herself as a giantess clinging to the Earth, stuck on, rubbing herself, stopping the planet's rotation and sinking down to the molten rock, who knows how far.

She no longer knows she's there, she's waited so long. She: nothing.

At the sound of the *dring* she is no longer disembodied. The ringing brings her to life again. Her head is throbbing unbearably. The atoms in her hand assemble on the receiver—it's her mother, or Delphine, and she's held fast by her own frustration.

Then she rescreens the movie of herself: she's a tiny pulsating speck in a village in a country in a continent, a miserable speck. Time has wound back to zero, no past, no future.

She remembers the words of her childhood prayer:

Hail Mary, full of grace, our Lord is with thee. Blessed art thou among women, and blessed is the fruit of thy womb, Jesus. Holy Mary, mother of God, make Arnaud call me, please Holy Mary, I'll do anything you want. Amen.

23 57 01

She lets it ring once and hangs up. The number is real. That has to be a sign.

'Come and set the table!' shouts Bihotz. The clanging of stainless steel cutlery.

She puts on a tape that Delphine made for her, turns

the volume up loud. She doesn't understand any of the lyrics but the music is all about her, her life. She presses her hands into her eyes and shakes her head around. Bihotz is there in a flash.

'For someone who has a migraine...'

She presses Pause and sighs, waiting for him to please go away and leave her alone. If her father is only a *porter*, she won't be getting a Walkman any time soon.

'If I'm so annoying, go home to your mother.'

He slams the door. Charming.

She is alone on the edge of the world. Cast out by some centrifugal force, alone, a long way from the centre where everything's happening.

23 57 01.

Just one ring. Hang up quickly.

23 57 01.

Just one more time.

'Hello.' A woman's voice. Annoyed. She picked up as soon as the ringtone started.

Is Arnaud there?

'Who is it?'

Her heart is pounding.

'Whom shall I say is calling?'

It looks like her porter father didn't teach her how to introduce herself.

It's Solange.

What a horrible name she has.

She hears the sound of a flute, 'Arnooooooo', an elegant, mocking flute.

She hangs up. She opens the window and looks down. It's only one storey but it's pretty high. Cement paving. There'd be a fair amount of damage. She should try it with Lulu.

The telephone rings. She makes herself wait for three rings. One. Two. Three.

Yes? It's more elegant than hello.

'Solange?'

Yes?

'Did you just call?'

No.

'My mother said it was Solange.'

No.

'Well, I only know one Solange…'

His deep voice, his voice that has two registers. Everything they've experienced together, every moment comes back to her, the blue bedroom and the river below. (Was it actually blue? With a Chinese screen.)

'Do you want to get together?'

Yes.

'When?'

Tomorrow?

'I can't tomorrow. The day after?'

*

Free.

She pedals as hard as she can. Town, silos, Milord's, marina. She heads off into the wind, into a blank space, without images, all speed, leaving behind her the places on a map. An enormous energy is coursing through her body, every push against the pedals is one more step towards far away, faster, a breakthrough.

On the promontory over the lake there is a statue of the Virgin Mary. Thank you, Mary, thanks for Arnaud's phone call. She has to go there with a pure heart, to appear as pure as possible before the goddess, who has X-ray vision and sees through our bodies right to the bottom of the cauldron that is our skull, focusing on our dreams and our desires like converging mirrors, amen. Because it's clear to Mary that she (Solange) is pure, as pure as when she was little (even purer, when she thinks now about what she thought about then).

She freewheels down to the river. Looks at the chateau on the opposite shore. Tries to locate the window. The balcony, on the top floor. The blue bedroom. Something's moving. Perhaps it's just a reflection in the windows—she had noticed there were cracks in the panes (when she stayed under the sheet struggling against the urge to go and join him straight away, to run after him).

As she cycles down along the shore, it really does look like something's moving. Lætitia d'Urbide? The servants? A rose garden. A tennis court. A swimming pool. An ensuite for each bedroom. *A dressing room.* There's even a *video room.*

And a leather lounge suite, pay by instalment. Designer carpet, cheaper by the yard.

Cheap Carpet—Lætitia d'Urbide, Lætitia d'U, Lady Di, Lady d'U.

Does she do it? Does she get like that too? Arched over and panting? *Penetrated? Possessed?* Does she make noises like on Canal+ TV? And Lady Di, does she?

Her mother. Her mother in that chateau. Waited on by servants. And why not? Her mother who drums into her that a woman must have a job. But the ideal would be not to work.

(Georges has a joke about sex on a posh couple's wedding night, it goes something like this—snobbish accent—'My dear, come in or go out but stop this ridiculous in and out business.')

And the word *fuckpad*, which a friend of Arnaud's used. Arnaud and this friend, seen from above when she was coming down the staircase. Their noses in their drinks, leaning in to each other. The friend had looked at her (arched over, panting) (as if he knew what she had just done, or not done).

Arnaud and her embracing, standing at the window. Lord and lady of their dominion.

Her arm around a tree like it's an imaginary body, her mouth open and sending kisses into the air, slightly arched over, slightly panting, glancing around to check that the foliage is hiding her.

*

She drops her bike and strides to the edge of the lake. Breathe and run. That's exactly what youth is, she thinks: grab and dash; it's fleeting, really fleeting, and hugely thrilling because it's NOW.

She has two days to lose two kilos. Once again she makes the solemn resolution not to eat anymore (only apples, tomatoes and cigarettes).

Georges is rigging windsurfers and there is absolutely no one else around. He says he can lend her a windsurfer and a wet suit. 'All those times I've offered you a go!'

She takes off her clothes as discreetly as possible behind the trailer. She hadn't thought about bringing her swimsuit so she puts the wetsuit on with nothing underneath and Georges tells her that it's not hygienic. 'Keep your underpants on. Who do you think you are, miss? I've seen plenty of *bums*.'

The wind is strong and steady towards the middle of the lake. She is hanging by both arms from the boom, the sail lifts her up, her feet are barely holding on and she charges straight ahead. She's so light. Lightly between sky and water. Anticipating the rhythm, bending her legs and absorbing the motion of the waves, taking off.

Back there the class has begun, four or five clowns and Georges like a king in his outboard, with his long blond hair, looking almost as good as her father. A big guy is with him, a distant cousin of Bihotz. She doesn't like him at all because he's always making idiotic jokes. And, sure enough, they head over in her direction. She has to turn around, *to go about*—but she falls in just when they get to her. Rusty-coloured slime oozes between her toes. Three mallards take off squealing and there are spiky reeds and the metallic taste of the water and the depressing absence of the sea.

'You okay?' asks Georges. Oddly enough, he offers her a cigarette. She takes one nonchalantly and pushes back a strand of wet hair. Everything's normal.

'It all depends on the positions'—the cousin is in full flight—'but I'm here to tell you that I was using my calorie-burning quota to the max, especially given what a sexpot the girl was.'

'He's doing Weight Watchers,' Georges translates.

'Three times,' continues the fat guy. 'Three times eight hundred calories makes two thousand four hundred calories—just watch how much weight I'm going to lose on this diet!'

They tow her out of the reeds and she can't wait for the day after tomorrow to come, so she can finally get back into her life.

Behind the trailer, she takes off the wetsuit and feels a weird warm spot. Did the rusty water seep inside? Blood. The wetsuit legs are full of it. What did she expect—there you go, it could only happen to her, her date is *the day after tomorrow* and she always gets it for at least five days.

Has it already been twenty-eight days since the last time? You could get your bearings if the calendar was in line with the moon, in girl months, and not their stupid imperial months of thirty or thirty-one days that get everything out of whack. Twenty-eight times thirteen makes exactly 364, plus an extra day for things like the 29th of February—so you can't say it doesn't work. If you followed that system you could actually organise dates.

She could have told him: *I can't the day after tomorrow.* Be mysterious, busy. *Next week, perhaps. If I'm free.*

'Be strategic. Be strategic,' Nathalie always says. Nathalie was the one who lent her a tampon, to try. But it hurt like hell, even after she dipped it in oil the way Nathalie told her to. Still, the fireman put a whole finger in there, and a finger is pretty big (and if you think about the other thing, about the size of it…better not to think about it). 'But you've got to be a bit wet,' explained Nathalie. 'That helps it slide in.'

She tried *masturbating* but even though she sighed, like her-mother-in-the-lotus-position, it didn't work. And anyway, Nathalie warned her about tampons: a girl forgot she had one in, and the guy pushed the tampon so far up her that it tore her insides and she died in a pool of blood.

Why is she crying tonight? She has no idea.

'I remember when I was your age, it wasn't easy, I had my ups and downs, they say it's the awkward age, my poor darling, but you can't stay a little girl all your life, you've got to find a way through it, you'll see, like a bed of thorns, and later you'll have a job, and children, you'll be fulfilled, you'll have a good life, better than mine, don't model yourself on me.'

She starts sobbing, distraught. Just having this conversation with her mother makes her hiccup. And—it happens every time—she says something she hadn't thought of saying, something she absolutely shouldn't say—that she knows the truth about Papa.

No reaction from her mother.

That Delphine said that Rose had seen him carrying suitcases. Papa.

As if it wasn't, like, the scoop of the century.

It was when they were going on holiday in England (she clarifies).

'Do you mean that Delphine said that Rose saw Papa looking after the suitcases of someone in particular?' Her mother manages to utter the words, with that frown on her forehead, as if her head was going to split in two.

She wants to press Rewind, it's the wrong conversation, the wrong runway for takeoff.

'Is that what you want to tell me?' insists her mother in this moment of *complicity* they're having. 'Is that why you're crying? Because Rose saw Papa with someone?'

She'd like to kill her.

Rose says that Papa is a porter.

Something like laughter appears in between the two pieces of her mother's face. She gets up to reheat the tisane of relaxing herbs that she leaves to infuse all day, and she massages her third eye with the tips of her fingers.

'When you were little,' she says from the kitchen, 'you always thought he was a pilot. Like in *The Little Prince*.'

Pilot or not, Papa is so much better looking than Maman…what's she on about? You've got to go out with someone in the same league as you. (Even if he was just a street-sweeper Solange would have married him, for sure.)

23.23 p.m.

It annoys her that Arnaud would think she's a virgin.

She slips on her sequinned T-shirt and tries it with her tube skirt. Or the jeans?

What she'd really like is if the barman or the DJ at Milord's kissed her in front of Arnaud. And served her that Pineapple-Malibu cocktail she likes—'the usual, Solange?' The DJ would put on 'Billie Jean', wink at her, and she'd dance like a goddess and everyone would look and Arnaud would come up to her but she would rebuff him gently—she likes to dance by herself—he'd try to steal a kiss from her and the fireman would knock him to the ground and the DJ and the barman would have to intervene, Arnaud would have a bloody nose, she would keep dancing then she'd agree to go home with him and she'd pull him against her groin, her mouth open and her pelvis thrusting, he'd lift up her skirt and pull down her shiny gym leggings and her underpants (or perhaps she'd be wearing just her Prince of Wales check skirt and underpants) and he would *penetrate* her on the bonnet of the car, she would be teetering on high heels, which would really help when she was arching her back (but if she's wearing jeans, is this actually possible when the jeans are pulled down?), and the fireman would be looking at them from the shadows, or (better?) the DJ and the barman would both be looking at her, they would think she was beautiful and a bit slutty, they would be jealous of Arnaud, she would open her mouth and arch backwards and Arnaud would slip his fingers between her teeth, she would bite them and groan and thrust her hips and hold him close (her arms folded over his back), wait, where would the fireman be (careful here), and Arnaud would *possess her violently*.

Once she's come (not very intense, the whole fantasy got a bit complex) she feels less like going out, but the idea of staying alone in her bedroom, of sleeping there after having *masturbated*, is so depressing.

Bihotz must be watching 'The Shrink Show'.

Her mother's dozed off. Solange pinches her high-heeled shoes and leaves quietly by the French window. She folds back the shutter. It creaks a bit but her mother's sleeping pills are the real deal.

Bihotz drives in silence. He hunches over the cigar lighter and smokes.

On the side of the road, the eyes of a paralysed rabbit.

He'd been sitting on his front steps. You'd think he was spying on her, or on the lookout for her or something.

'Were you really going to the airport?'

Yes.

A night bird grazes the bonnet of the car.

'What do you want with your father?'

To see him take off.

'On the last plane?' He says that like it was a joke. Anyway, he's taken the road to the airport.

She would have liked to go to the sea. Drive to the sea at night. She could have said to him: I've never seen the sea at night. It would have been true, and like in a film. Black waves. She would have had that feeling of finally being in the right film.

She wonders what he's thinking about. It's a bit of a freak-out to even think that. She slides a Marlboro out of the pack, puts it between her lips and lights it.

With a wave of his hand he knocks the cigarette away. She screams and twists around all over the place. It smells of scorched carpet, but her T-shirt is untouched.

You were already smoking when you were twelve, she protests. *You used to hide in the chicken coop.*

'I was smoking when I changed your nappies. I filled your bum with smoke, if you really want to know.'

Go to hell.

What brilliant repartee. She takes another cigarette

and feels invincible. There's a cassette sticking out of the car radio, she pushes it in and it's the band that Delphine recorded for her.

'We've come to play in the happy house. We're in a dream in the happy house...'

He's singing over the top of the girl's voice. With a really good accent.

So you're stealing my cassette tapes?

'I have a very broad taste in music.'

You don't know anything.

She blows out the smoke and if he doesn't watch out they'll end up in the fucking ditch.

She watches him carefully. Only last week he took out a membership at the music section of the local library. And he's a fanatic at Gym Tonic. Because, go figure, he might have a girlfriend. That'd be funny.

You've never even slept with a girl, never even touched one.

To sound nastier, she'd have to say *tu* and not *vous*. Virgin. Faggot. Prick. The ruder, the funnier.

'What would you know?'

I'm always here.

'Not all the time.'

Stop the bullshit. At your age it's totally embarrassing. I wouldn't want to be in your shoes. If I were you, I wouldn't even dare *leave the house.*

He stops under a tree and she's a bit frightened again. He cuts the motor and silence descends. There's a strange vibe coming off him, as if he doesn't quite inhabit the same time zone as her, as if he knows things she doesn't know. And what she wants is to drive fast, to go towards something, in the future, further away, the sea.

I mean, you never go out. You can't live like that. Even my mother says it—and my mother adores you. She says life is passing you by.

He leans over, takes her cigarette between his thumb and index finger, throws it away. Everything goes very slowly and she doesn't utter a word. They look at each other. He grabs her shoulders with both hands and she feels small and very strong. He leans over, a thread of vapour separates them, time suspended in tenderness. But he sits back. Starts the engine again. The music blares.

Rising through the darkness, broken only by the beam of the headlights, is a glow that is neither sunset nor dawn, but the airport.

'There's something you need to know.'

As if she didn't already know everything.

One day she saw a porter, in a train station. The only time she's taken a train. It looked like begging was part of his job. She couldn't care less about her father. She never wants to work. Ever.

'You are in love with your father.'

She bursts out laughing. *That's* what he wants to tell her?

'You haven't *thought* about things enough. There are connections between things, connections that you might not have seen. It's what's called the butterfly effect. When a butterfly flutters its wings in China, there are repercussions as far as Clèves. It's the same thing in your life. Things that happened a long time ago or that your grandparents did or even people who lived during the Middle Ages but who are linked to you through pathways that you could not begin to imagine. It's the same thing with your father. And you have to work on this, very methodically, free your mind of it. Otherwise, you know what will happen? You're going to throw yourself on the first guy who fronts up. All because you're in love with your father. It's the inner tyrant.'

The in-her what?

'The inner tyrant.'

She's laughing so much she's crying. Her head out the window, breathing big gulps of balmy air.

'It's like your father's inside you and is masterminding you. He *makes* you do things but you don't even realise. It's very, very common, especially for girls. You internalise your inner tyrant so much that you become your own inner tyrant.'

Like a tapeworm?

'A what?'

If you swallow one that's in bread that a pig has pissed on, afterwards it makes you eat things you don't want to eat.

There's an awkward silence.

It's something I read. Anyway, it might be true.

He's big, hairy, familiar and, watching him drive, she thinks that yes, amazingly, he does have something of her father about him. Or her father has something of Bihotz about him. Now she'd like to apologise. For having made fun of him.

What would you have wanted to do—for a job?

She'd like to have a serious conversation and another cigarette.

'If what?'

I dunno. If you had worked.

'What do you think I'm doing with you?'

It's not a job.

'Well, what do you think it is?'

I don't know. A mission?

He laughs. It's funny how talking to him makes her more *spiritual*, as if she knows he'll always approve of her.

There's a plane on the runway. It's the Caravelle flight to Paris. People are walking under the wing and they could be wearing hats and trench coats like in the olden days, or pink suits like that woman trying to protect her blood-drenched husband in the convertible. They've been leaving for Paris forever, boarding in the timeless night-time.

'What'll we do? Will we get on? Go to Paris together?'

She laughs.

Through the automatic glass door she thinks she glimpses her father, straight ahead, behind an Air Inter counter. In his uniform and cap. The door opens him up into two and vaporises him at the edges, then he comes together again, scarcely disturbed at all, resuming his conversation with a flickering air hostess. It's him, it's her father. Her father is an air hostess—she realises she's always known it—whatever you call the men, steward, ground steward, at the check-in desk.

Time: parallel lines of unequal width along an undulating, hazy ribbon. And there's another dimension, which is not space, not airports or the sky, but a sort of pit, in which her father goes up and down—pilot, porter, a pea in a lift—yo-yoing in this secret passage, smuggled into the *upper classes.*

And a bit later, sitting in the J7, she sees him opening the door of the Alpine for the air hostess, she sees him as if for the first time, tall, svelte, elegant, almost like in an advertisement, a man who is her father, a man who calls himself her father, that man there in the car park.

Arnaud is supposed to be coming to pick her up on his moped. She's waiting for him out the front of her place, between the two houses, holding a helmet Bihotz made her take that dates back to when he had a moped.

It's four o'clock. Tea time. Her mother is at the shop. No chance Arnaud will catch sight of her. It would be embarrassing if he saw Bihotz, but *she couldn't care less about Bihotz.*

A dramatic expression on her face, the helmet in her hand, standing in the sun, jiggling from one foot to the other in her black outfit (her father's Polo and a pencil skirt and a little gold chain she bought at Dames de France and mascara and a black Borsalino hat she found in the cellar, never worn but classy in the most totally natural way). It's the dramatic expression she's practised in front of the mirror but perhaps it conveys the truth about her. She wore black because she's dark and mysterious, and a little gold chain because she's chic. What sort of girl is she *really* and which is cooler, to be *damaged* or *dependable*? Solange is dependable, Solange is in a bad way, Solange is very stable, Solange plays her cards close to her chest, Solange is perverse—it reminds her of the *Martine* magazines she read when she was little.

She's in black because she's on her own, an orphan, and because if there's a leak, the blood will be less visible.

At 4.15 Bihotz is smoking on his front steps and calls out to say what a great spot it is for a breath of fresh air. The guy thinks he's so smart.

This morning she read her erotic horoscope in one of her mother's magazines. 'Venus is in your sign and you will be ruled by your desire. Your partner, under the influence of Mars governed by Saturn, is likely to be amazed but no more than you would expect. Surprising combinations are not to be ruled out. You will be transformed into a powerful horsewoman and it will be Love itself that you be astride. Drunk with sensuality, overflowing with passion, you will not know which way to turn to satisfy your admirer. Ice is not your element and you will burn under the tender gaze of Love.'

'Aren't you hot in black?'

What a moron.

She's going to smell sweaty. As she stands in the blazing sun the sanitary napkin fills up bit by bit and that's going to stink too. What a drag. How many more years before she's rid of it? Thirty at least. If not forty.

Love itself. Under the tender gaze of Love.

It's going to take a while getting to the coast on the moped. She hasn't said anything to Bihotz (that Arnaud lives so far away) and how is she going to manage with her hat? Helmet plus hat, she hadn't thought about that.

Actually it's worked out quite well. The bleeding. She won't do it this time. According to Nathalie, you shouldn't sleep with a guy the first time, or the second time, or the third time. From the fourth time on, okay. By then the guy has shown that he'll pay the price. You've got to get him to respect you.

4.20. Still sitting out the front of his place, Bihotz is waving a piece of string while Lulu jumps at it like an arthritic cat.

She's not sure whether Arnaud is the type to wait. She's not sure whether she's worth waiting for that many times. It's hard to believe there are girls who are still virgins at twenty. How excruciating.

Bihotz shouts something else in her direction, waggling rabbit ears with his fingers.

Idiot.

On the other hand, Nathalie says that doing it while you've got it is the best form of contraception. Apparently the blood kills the sperm. Whatever, getting pregnant the first time you did it would be like losing at Russian roulette.

A faint buzzing in the distance, a moped, the noise gets louder and Bihotz yells, 'HERE HE COMES!'

There he is. He's here.

Hi, she says casually. He turns so she can give him a peck on both cheeks (a bad sign?).

She straddles the luggage carrier, Bihotz yells something else (he's tapping his head: the helmet), she jams her hat under her bum and sticks the thing on her head, she's going to have flat hair, what was the point of teasing it. She looks behind her for somewhere to hold on, Arnaud calls out something to her, she puts her arms around him, at first loosely then (it goes fast) right up close, and the Borsalino flies off.

He brakes. Stops. 'Lean into the corners. Can't you feel it? If you don't lean you'll tip us over.'

She's such an idiot.

Anyway, it was just an old hat from the cellar.

Corner after corner, and the insides of her thighs are really starting to chafe, but he stops suddenly in front of a house (they are nowhere near the coast). Arnaud kicks out the stand, *clack*, takes off his helmet and shakes out his hair, the light sparkles in his green eyes and he looks so *mature*.

They climb a staircase, a voice calls out, 'Arnooooo?'

But he shuts the door. There are posters of Corto Maltese and of bands she doesn't know, and an entire wall of Polaroids—him and a whole bunch of people.

He gestures to her. 'Can you put on the record?' He actually has a stereo in his room.

She concentrates on getting the stylus in the groove of the 45; it jumps.

'Be careful!'

She starts again; that's it.

He tries to play along with the solo on his guitar.

Anyway, she shouldn't kid herself, they're just going to have a hot chocolate or something.

There's a knock at the door.

'Yeeessss?' (He imitates a woman's voice, it's so funny.)

A loose perm and a bat-wing shirt and two hands carrying a tray with two orange juices—that's all she can see because Arnaud is blocking the doorway and saying, Yes, it's Solange and yes, hello, 'say hello, Solange', *hello*, 'hello, *Madame*', *hello, Madame*, 'you have to be told how to do everything'. He laughs and she laughs too and the phantom disappears.

He turns up the music and locks the door. Something about this gesture grabs her. That bolt in its cylinder: just the two of them, all by themselves.

She sips her juice without making a sound, so refined.

He mumbles over his chords.

'Fuck!' He throws down the guitar. He stretches. 'Look at the Ramones, or even Johnny Rotten, not one of them knows how to play. It's *energy*, that's what counts. Rebellion.'

He lights a cigarette. In his bedroom. With his mother just downstairs.

'Rebellion. You know what? *Rebellion* (he puts on a serious voice) is a huge piece of commercial dishonesty. They lie, you buy. Open your eyes and you'll see how lies are the basis of our society. Take my mother. Do you think that's the real colour of her hair? It's all social conditioning. And you're conditioned, too—to want one thing and not another. You know what? You lie to yourself—you've been conditioned so much. All because why? So you'll want to buy stuff. Stuff you don't *need*. So that you'll want to *buy yourself, buy you*. Okay, the Ramones, they're for real. But not Johnny Rotten. Not anymore. *No way*.'

He opens a window, grabs a pair of jeans off the floor and waves them in the air. She gets that it's to clear the smoke and she grabs a T-shirt and waves it around too.

'As for my mother, perhaps that's not even her *real body*. Perhaps that's an alien conditioned to look like my real mother, who is wandering around somewhere after she's been brainwashed...No kidding, it pisses me off that she won't buy me a car. I'm eighteen in five and a half months, I'm not going to spend the rest of my life on a moped.

It's insane. Stop doing that with the T-shirt.'

He sprays perfume round the room and puts some under his arms. *Azzaro for Men.* It's heavenly. Like a forest with sweetener added. Azzaro for Arnaud. He sits on the bed and pats the spot next to him. A cabin bed with drawers underneath. He smiles. 'So do I have to do everything?' He kisses her. He pushes her onto the crumpled sheets and blankets. He whispers in her ear. That he is shy and he needs some affection.

I have to go to the toilet.

He unlocks the door. Luckily there's a basin and she washes herself without splashing too much water everywhere. There shouldn't be blood again straight away. She wishes she could call Nathalie to ask what she would do now.

She's got lines of some kind on her inner thighs. She's never noticed them before. They must be *stretch marks.* It's ridiculous. A ride on the back of a moped was all it took for the skin over her flesh to crack?

What to do with the pad? There's a rubbish bin, of course, a ceramic frog with a lily-pad lid. But they'd know who put it there. She rolls it up tight inside some toilet paper. There's no pocket in her skirt. She hides it in her fist. Pulls the chain—it's decorated with a macramé cap. Flips down the lid—it's also covered with a sort of tapestry material. The flush makes a hell of a noise.

She's startled—the mother is right there, outside the toilet door.

'I knew it wasn't Arnaud. He never pulls the chain. Do you need anything? Is everything okay?'

Yes. No.

She goes back up the stairs, she'd like to run but that would be weird in front of the mother, and she's frightened she'll leak. She squeezes her hand tight over the pad, it barely sticks out at all.

Arnaud has put the record back on. He hugs her and she'd like to hug him too but she's only got one free hand and there's the helmet, right there—she'll hide the pad inside, under the visor. She manages to do it by wriggling around and there's a sort of quid pro quo, he kisses her on the nape of her neck, he lifts up her skirt and rubs his dick against her underpants. There's blood. Shit, there's blood. There's definitely *nothing* she can do, but he already has his fingers in her underpants.

'Don't pull that trick on me again. You've actually got to do it the first time if you want to do it a second time.'

Fair enough. But it's not that, it's not that she's never done it before—he must definitely not think that—it's just that (watch out, she's going to say it, it's her turn, sad and serious) *I am indisposed.*

'Indisposed for what? You mean like girls?'

He pulls his hand back as if it's been bitten. He holds his bitten hand in front of him and unlocks the door again. She can hear the water running in the bathroom.

'Arnooooo? Do you need anythiiiiing?'

She wipes herself with the sheet. Perhaps she should leave. Despite what her horoscope says. But if she goes home early, that would make Bihotz's day.

Arnaud comes back with the same look he had when he stuck his moped on the stand even though they weren't at the coast. A *mature* look. He locks the door again.

Fuck the horoscope. And fuck Bihotz. She leans over, lets herself fall onto the bed, he follows her, it's sweet, tender, they're lying on their sides like teaspoons. A long cuddle. She tilts her neck so that he can kiss her nape again, he rubs himself against her buttocks. She feels so happy. It's heavenly. All those painful years were worthwhile because of this single moment, this moment she was always destined for. That whole interminable past is emerging from an airless fog the colour of lake water and reeds, the slime of her infancy.

He sits up for a second to raise the volume, his dick is sticking out level with the record, as if he was playing it with the end of his penis. A musical penis. A penis with a stylus.

He lies down like a teaspoon again. She feels something really weird, something not at all *normal* but he hugs her very hard, she screams *stop* and he stops.

'It's best like that. The best thing to do. Since you can't do it.'

Huh?

'Don't make me spell out everything. It's annoying. We can, like, communicate without words. You girls have a very different relationship with your bodies. Straightforward.

Whereas we guys need a bit more (he hesitates), a bit more time and tact from you. For example, people have been doing that forever. It's a cultural given. In the old days the Greeks did it all the time because the girls wanted to stay virgins, and right now, for example, I'm not criticising you, but since you don't want to, that is we can't, anyway it's easy, getting it to slip in I mean, so first you have to suck me and then it'll go in by itself.'

So first she has to suck him. The record stops, she gets (he gestures with his hand) that she has to start the music again. Keeping the dick in her mouth, she grabs the arm of the record player and tries to aim for the right groove while balancing on an elbow, it's not easy. 'Come on,' she hears, 'get going, it's killing me.' She feels a hot trickle between her legs. It's going to stain the carpet. Loose-perm is not going to be happy. The record starts up again, she's going to end up knowing it better than 'Billie Jean', she should try to read the name of the band but it's spinning too quickly.

The dick slips out of her mouth. He groans—stuff it back in. There's something tickling at the back of her throat. She starts coughing and the blood spurts and she tries to stop it with her hand between her legs, she coughs and stops sucking for a second. He looks at her, gobsmacked. It's a pubic hair. Frizzy. No wonder it tickled. She gets back to it, her mouth busy and her hand too, between her legs, it feels good, she goes hard at it, come on, no slacking.

But he pushes her off, shuts his eyes and does yoga-style

breathing (she wipes herself with the sheets). What does she do now, what does she do with all these bits of body—put them together again. An explosion—it would be good to have an *orgasm.*

'Okay,' he whispers.

On all fours behind her, he really does look like a dog. She sticks close to him so he won't see the blood (and the stretch marks). As long as they stay cuddled up like that it's fine, but all of a sudden (what a shock) it slides inside her. In that hole. Let's be clear about this: in the poo hole. The pain shoots right through her. He's holding on hard to her buttocks and saying something like, 'Oohh, that's so good.' He repeats it and adds, 'little bitch.' For once he seems to be speaking without irony. And the words are going inside there too, and it feels really odd and tight, irritating but not unpleasant, it's as if it's getting bigger bit by bit, something gets hot and stiff and feels pretty good (not the dick, it's her, her own body, *right there*).

She lowers her head and looks between her legs. She has balls. Balls hanging down from her and swinging, *gling glong.* Pink and hairless, like her thighs, which are looking pretty good from this angle, slim, toned, strong, and her belly and her two little breasts and the feeling of being immense, spread out like a countryside, and of having this hanging thing bobbing around, a grasshopper, that's it, a big field and a little grasshopper.

Leaning further down, her buttocks in the air and her

forehead on the mattress (if Bihotz could see her) she can see the dick clearly, it's funny, a snout nuzzling her, a long sausage body with a cloud of curly pubic hair—with the few pubic hairs she has it's like a poodle shaved everywhere except the head and the bum. A poodle that gets longer and then shorter, a poodle on a spring, *dzoing, dzoing.*

He straightens her up, pulling on her hips and making a rasping sound. He's clutching at her, it's getting unpleasant. She tries to rub herself against something. She doesn't dare put her hands down there, apparently (Nathalie says) real women orgasm without using their hands (even *doing this*?). She lowers her buttocks and looks for a pillow or a bunched-up blanket, it's not much fun—no, the shooting pain is too awful.

Stop.

Stop!

'What?'

Stop, please. It's hurting a bit.

'But I've almost finished, oh, please, oh wow, I've almost finished.' His sentence is lost as he keeps moving, it really does hurt, she should relax (Nathalie says that frigid women don't know how to relax), fortunately it doesn't last and exactly at the moment when the record stops he lets out a dreadful cry.

She listens out for Loose-perm but there's no sign of her. It's leaking everywhere now, she makes do with the sheet, and while he seems to be sleeping (or recovering?) she finds her pad in the helmet and sticks it back in her underpants, quickly, and pulls her skirt down and starts to pant like him, to give the right impression.

She puts her head gently on his shoulder and they stay there like that, he calms down, she shuts her eyes and sees the blue bedroom with the Chinese screen and the window open onto the river and how the hot wind wafted over their faces.

'How are you getting home?' asks Arnaud. He's doing up the buttons of his 501s.

She had thought that he might take her home, or that they might go for a walk together (by the sea), but she just has to make a call (to Bihotz) and *Someone's coming to get me.*

'Don't stress,' says Arnaud.

She's in Loose-perm's car and the countryside is unfolding in reverse, lake–river–Milord's–Cheap Carpet–silos. He didn't say when he'd call her again.

'Are you okay? You look wistful.'

I'm okay. Her bottom is a bit sore.

'Are you hungry? There's some chocolate in the glove box.'

No thanks. She'd like to get home quickly and wash herself.

'I do like it when Arnaud's girlfriends come over, it brightens things up round the house. Arnaud doesn't have a sister, it's my biggest regret. I had such a dreadful time when he was born—I tore terribly, from my anus to my clitoris, months and months of incontinence—I didn't want to have any more children. It's sad, but that's the way it is.'

Fortunately there's no way she could be pregnant. And that disease her father was talking about, it takes two years, or three, and it's probably not that easy to catch. She'd be in high school or even older, she'd be grown up, *a young woman*, and where would she be? She would have already lived a whole life. Perhaps with Arnaud? The entire future contained in those two unending years.

'I wouldn't exchange Arnaud for anything in the world, it's just I would have liked to have a girl as well. Come over whenever you want to, I'll come and get you and I'll bring you home. The bike is dangerous with two people on it. I've told Arnaud but he takes no notice.'

The helmet? What's she done with Bihotz's helmet?

'People are stupid when they live alone. Arnaud's father...I know your mother, she's got the souvenir shop in Clèves-le-Haut, she's told me that it's difficult with your father too. Your mother has great taste but she has no way to express herself, that's the tragedy with women. Your generation has to continue the battle, carry on what we started.'

Perhaps he'll call her about the helmet.

Bihotz is out the front of his place. Suddenly it's like she can see old Madame Bihotz there, huge and hunched, she's been growing there forever, lichen for hair and a skull and crossbones on her biceps. And while he chats to

Arnaud's mother, he's different again, he looks virile and responsible and a bit alarming and he looks at her as if he was deciphering her, half challenging her, half concerned, and she wonders: is that what it is, *to be fucked?* Or *raped*, is that what it is? Technically, was that my *first time*? She has to work it out before she tells Nathalie all about it.

III

DOING IT AGAIN

She doesn't know what to do with her arms. They've sprung out of her body and she's lugging them around attached to her shoulders. They used to follow her when she moved. Now she's been landed with arms that have heads on the ends. She's got them to worry about as well as her face. Hand-faces that she has to monitor as if several other Solanges had been joined onto her. She'd look self-conscious if she put them in her pockets. But taking them out means everyone will see these long creatures that have nothing to do with her and yet are horribly dependent on her, and everything she's thinking (which is nothing, except for her embarrassment) will be exposed, twitching, right down to her fingernails.

The folk dancers in the horse costumes are jumping as high as they can. Girls in red and white dresses are twirling round and round a flagpole, plaiting and unplaiting ribbons. Nathalie is playing the recorder and Concepción the tambourine.

Everyone is looking at what she, Solange, is doing with her hands. To see if she knows what to do with her body, this beaten-up body, that she wants to roll up in a ball and hide away and live without.

'Stand up straight,' sighs her mother. 'Stop acting like a baby. Look at Concepción, such lovely poise.'

Bihotz's cousin is getting married. They're lucky, it's a beautiful day. Her father hasn't come. He hasn't been home for a few days. She has to stand up straight and smile, be a good advertisement for the shop. Her mother put eye shadow on her. They chose a mauve mascara from the Rimmel range. Then she wiped it all off in front of the mirror with cottonwool dipped in Embryolisse cleanser, while her mother yelled that they were going to be late. And she did it all again, exactly the same but by herself, pink eye shadow and the mauve mascara.

If her father was here he'd flash his dick again.

Christian and Rose are sitting on the stand opposite. Holding hands. So what. She saw Arnaud at the wedding reception. The sight of him (nobody wears 501s like he does) made her heart leap.

'You don't have to turn your nose up like that,' says her mother. 'All right, it might not be a Cure concert'—she pronounces it *kiiyure*—'but they're local traditions and they're worthy of respect. They're part of who we are. It's where we come from.' Her mother has started to relearn the local language. Apparently her grandparents spoke only Basque, not even French or anything.

Monsieur Bihotz is very cheerful. He's with Delphine and her mother and the cousin's mother. She's given up trying to understand the connections in this *tentacular* family. In the early days of Clèves there must have been Bihotz stock that began the line and then they all reproduced among themselves. Just look how he's joking with Delphine and her cow of a mother. He's got on a suit she's never seen before, and he's actually wearing a *bowtie*.

'For heaven's sake, what is the matter with you?' grumbles her mother. 'Do you think it's easy for me, in front of everyone? I should have asked Monsieur Bihotz to come with us. People take advantage of a woman without a man.'

Once the show's over, the breeze wafting through the stands makes her mother flutter like a curtain. She dreamed up the idea of having the local dressmaker make two matching harem-pants jumpsuits in Liberty print (how hysterical this morning when she accidentally put on Solange's oufit!). She made Solange add a mauve crossover top because the weather is cool for this time of year. Is it all because Papa is not around? Her mother doesn't usually behave like this. She doesn't jiggle from one foot to the other.

Actually everyone is really weird. They're all dressed up as if they're waiting for the giant spaceship that will take them into outer space. All of Clèves will blast off except for her. Her mother will scream out: 'Solange!' Or Bihotz will. No, he's too busy *flirting* with Delphine's mother.

Planet Clèves 2000.

Bihotz's cousin has lost a lot of weight. And the bride is not the bombshell they were expecting. She's just a new Madame Bihotz, wrapped up in whipped cream with a veil and high heels. As if the name just flipped from one woman to the other. And Monsieur Bihotz, best man, playing the suitor. The groomsmen are all wearing formal suits. It's grotesque.

Georges is the civil witness (he's with his girlfriend and their little boy, who is also wearing a bowtie). When their eyes meet, he gives her a smile, but he's not really going to see her, and her mother isn't going to see him either. And she doesn't know what to do, what to say, and her hands are getting heavier still on the ends of her arms.

Oh, to be a child again. When she was little, the external world didn't seem to weigh so heavily on the surface of her being. She grew up without having to force her way out, like a plant into the open air. Without spilling out of herself under the crushing weight of the world. She would like to slide in between the cracks like a seed, grow differently, somewhere else.

The photographer tells them to say cheese. '*Ouistiti!* Not *cheese*,' the mayor calls out. 'We're in France, here!' Everyone laughs, click, and Monsieur and Madame the Baron d'Urbide arrive. They don't want to intrude, they shake hands with the bride and groom, their daughter Lætitia still dressed in black, with enormous buckled shoes and unbelievable fingerless lace gloves.

'She's completely crazy, that chick! Comes to a wedding dressed like a widow…' sniggers one of the Lavinasse women, pregnant for most of the last few years.

Arnaud is over there, on the other side of the stands. If he sees her with her mother, there'll be a midair collision. *It was my father who died*, she'll explain. *I couldn't care less about my mother.* She'll have a sublime expression on her face that'll make him fall silent, moved by her suffering. Sublime in her floral harem pants and mauve crossover.

'Are you listening to me?' grumbles her mother. 'Or does everything always have to revolve around you?'

The two mothers get together at the beginning of the reception dinner. They went to school together at Sainte-Marie-du-Bas-Bourg.

'Your son is lovely,' sighs her mother. You can see her bra through the Liberty print.

Arnaud keeps going backwards and forwards between the tables. Her mother stares at him, it's really embarrassing. As if her mother was calling up some inner landscape, some immense mental wasteland of her own. Where Solange has no place. Her mother's trying to look intriguing. Or she's had too much to drink. She herself has managed to drink four glasses of wine, right under her mother's nose.

She'd prefer to not even think about the wedding cake, about the puff pastries stacked up there in the caramel, a landslide of puff pastry for anyone to eat. After she's stuffed herself with all the crazy salads, the vol-au-vents, the jellied salmon, the apple granita, the ox tongue in capers, the curly endive salad with diced ham and the vast array of cheeses. For two days she'd managed to eat only tomatoes.

'These children only think about themselves,' says Arnaud's mother. 'I can't begin to tell you. I know what you've been through. How brave of you. You and your husband. Such a good man.'

Her mother smiles her shopkeeper's smile. Actually she's really out of it. Bernadette of Lourdes at the cave. Tonight she'll go to bed with two Valium and three Di-gesics.

Arnaud is talking with Delphine and Lætitia d'Urbide. Apparently they're going on to Milord's because the music here is so atrocious (The Chicken Dance). That's the very moment Bihotz chooses to ask her for a dance, 'Come on Solange,' with that accent that just swallows her name, his yawning 'o' and 'an' sounds, Salaannngeuh.

Instead she asks for a coffee (her very first coffee). Lukewarm, bitter, horrible. 'So you drink coffee now?'—Bihotz laughs and so does Delphine's mother. What's so funny? They go off dancing.

'Monsieur Bihotz looks like he's full of beans,' her

mother manages to say. Then she nods off, her chin in her bra, a landslide like the wedding cake.

The bride is a bit dishevelled, she's pulled off her veil, her hair looks like Concepción's on her first day at school, but her ringlets are mussy, bobbing around, she seems completely happy, completely fulfilled, married for better or for worse, before the *honeymoon.* ('All of a sudden she was gripped by a sharp pain; and she started groaning, writhing in his arms, while he possessed her violently.') (But surely they've already slept together, even if she is wearing white.)

Arnaud has moved right in close to Lætitia d'Urbide and Solange knows what that's about, she's already seen it with Rose and Christian. Yes, and between her father and the pharmacy woman too, and her father and the air hostess. And other women, come to think of it.

She takes a pastry, swiftly, discreetly. Delphine's mother is laughing so loudly you can hear her shrieks above the music, shrieks emerging from her wide-open mouth, out of her plump little body in Bihotz's clutches.

Legs leaping, dresses ballooning, hands stretched out and squeezing each other. She wipes her fingers on the tablecloth. She feels too solidly grounded and, at the same time, as if she's been turned to vapour, unable to stay within the boundary of her own body or even stay in a particular spot in the room. What should she do about this huge void, inside her, devouring her? She could smoke and drink and eat and swallow, fill herself up with the whole wedding banquet, with the whole village, with everything that's missing—and everything would still be missing.

She thinks about the cream puff pastries and about Arnaud. About Arnaud and the cream puff pastries. They are superimposed over each other, so filling, so hideously desirable. To love is to want to breathe the air the other person breathes (or something like that). She gets up and heads towards him, between the tables.

He yells out: 'Angie!'

He pronounces it Heyndjiii. No one has ever called her that. It's so sexy and rock'n'roll. So not Solange. So *it.* It's the name of that girl who is hidden inside her, buried under the sticky girl full of pastry. Angie, whom he, Arnaud, can see.

And apparently Lætitia can too. She's inexplicably friendly. As if they've known each other forever. Or rather, no—quite the reverse—as if Lætitia was discovering her, Angie, the girl behind Solange. And she's instantly in agreement—at how dumb this party is and how dumb it is to get married. And how dumb Arnaud is too, with his new haircut, short at the front and long behind; just because it's fashionable doesn't mean it suits him.

So liberated, this Lætitia. So unconventional. She's got to stop saying *so*. Stop saying words like that. Angie is a cool, liberated girl who has no verbal tics and who absolutely could not care less about fashion, *fashion is about dictatorship.*

Lætitia has some dope. They go out to smoke a joint and Lætitia trips on the step, laughing at herself, reaching out her long gloved hands so she can be helped up, so she can be taken out of the diaphanous contraption of her unbelievable clothes, tulle, leather, lace and metal, a bride in a black jumble of clothes, an *antidote*, the word pops into Solange's head. Antidote yourself, she starts giggling, they fall and collapse on each other in a fit of laughter, one wearing flowers, the other in black, they roll around like rugby players.

'She really is drunk,' Arnaud observes.

We all are, says Solange, super-witty. Lætitia screams with laughter.

It's like a magnetic storm, something has shifted, the party's turned around, the night has brightened up, what was horrible is becoming wonderful.

Arnaud holds out his hand, to her, to Solange, she grabs it, lifts herself up, one foot on top of the other, boom boom, hippopotamus yourself. He looks at her intensely.

She tries to look as *cool* as possible. To look like she's done it a whole heap of times, without necessarily looking like a *slut*. Neither a slut nor a virgin. Pure. To look super-sensual but fragile, too, like Kim Wilde. To look like she hasn't been drinking.

She hiccups a bit more laughter. That look of his… All of Arnaud is in that look. That face leaning in. And that cologne of his, their past, their whole history together is coming back…

'What's that purple stuff you've got on your eyelashes?'

She opens her eyes wide.

'You matched your eye make-up with your outfit? That is particularly vulgar. Vulgar in the extreme.'

A slow afternoon at Monsieur Bihotz's. He's weeding the moss in the corner of the garden; she's complaining about not going to the sea.

'If there was a tidal wave,' says Bihotz, 'we'd be very glad to be living here.' He stands up, red, sweaty, wearing a bucket hat on his oval head, on top of his huge body: she sees a dick, a big, shiny dick tied up in gardening gear.

She must be sick.

When she was little, they used to trace their fingers along the contour lines on road maps, imagining the sea rising everywhere, bays in plains, fjords in valleys. How could she have been interested in such silly stuff? She has no idea.

At lunchtime he cooks rabbit. But why not cat or dog? He waited until she wasn't around so he could kill it without her crying and carrying on. Without her chaining herself to the hutch like those militant anti-abortionists who chain themselves to operating tables (so Rose's mother told her).

Madame Bihotz used to break their necks on the corner of a table. She doesn't want to know how he does it. He's having one of his bad days. And he's carrying on with that *mystical* stuff, as Rose would say. He says: 'Sometimes I get the feeling people get me mixed up with the Boursenave kid. Sometimes I get the feeling people think I'm the village idiot. I live very differently from the way they do, with their pathetic imitation bodies.'

Your problem is that you didn't manage to hook up with Delphine's mother.

She always needs to torment him. She couldn't care less about him, even less than her parents! But as soon as she manages to upset him, to *wound* him, it's like she's frightened he won't love her anymore. But there's no way he could stop loving her. And when she thinks it through like that, all by herself in her own mind, it's amazing how adult she feels. It's so much easier than when she speaks. Much easier than if she has to *explain herself*. For example, with Arnaud. (With Bihotz she manages, sometimes.)

'And you, Solange,' he says suddenly (with the same speedy repartee as her), 'did you manage to hook up with Arnaud?'

Fair enough. She's amazed he remembered his name. Since the wedding, she dials his number a hundred times a day. Without lifting up the receiver. 23 57 01. Then she goes numb. She stays sitting in front of the telephone.

Bihotz is drinking a beer in the kitchen and she gets one too. He looks preoccupied, he wouldn't notice anything. It can't be Delphine's mother who's put him in this mood. He's taken off his gardening gear and underneath he's wearing his wolf T-shirt, a T-shirt that her father (or Georges, or

Arnaud) would never be seen dead in, the same T-shirt as the fireman. That was so long ago.

It's sunny in front of the window and her eyes are half-closed.

Billie Jean. Hard lips, groping hands. The wolf, his neck craning in the direction of Milord's disco ball. Time is a tiny mirror drifting off the disco ball, approaching, spinning. Sequins and bass guitar. Lips, hands, *Billie Jean*. And that unbelievable gesture, that finger jammed in there—she can hear her own voice. *Stop, please. It hurts a bit.* Remembered voices, remembered bodies, all merging together. She has to stop the cursor from moving, stabilise time and find herself a body to kiss again (in the past she used to call it going out with a boy).

Bihotz gets another beer.

Try again. Lips, hands. Shut your eyes. Has it worn out? Can time wear out, from passing, from remembering, like records, does time leave dust motes that get in your eyes? She feels weak, dizzy. (*So sappy*, her father would say, sniggering.)

I really like your T-shirt.

'Why can't you say *tu*?'

Why would I use the familiar form with you?

'I really like YOUR—*familiar form*—fucking T-shirt. And call me by my fucking first name.'

Her eyes are prickling. She has a lump in her throat. She takes another beer, he doesn't say anything. She no longer knows what day it is out there, outside. The days unfold with no other purpose than to carry her, like a train, towards a destination where she will finally be free. She hates it when he's nasty. When he pretends nothing's wrong. Pretends not to see her. She goes over and sits in his lap, straddling his knees.

Stay calm, Monsieur Bihotz. She places her lips on his lips. It's not at all like it was with the fireman. She suddenly feels extremely happy. *Stay calm*, it pops out from between her teeth while she concentrates on kissing him again.

He stays so calm he's like a log of wood. The only part of him that's moving is right there, in his work overalls, it's getting bigger.

She sits back a bit and looks at him. His eyes are closed and his mouth is half-open. She knows him so well that she can't see him, can't see him *objectively.* The wolf is moving up and down on his chest. The enormous moon on the T-shirt folds and unfolds, the material splitting into little flakes. He washes everything too hot, at 90 degrees. She settles against his belly, peels off a piece of the moon, and wiggles her hips slowly.

'Stop,' he says. His dick sticking up like a pyramid under his overalls. His eyes still shut. If he opens them, she'll stop. If he keeps them shut, she'll keep going.

She pushes her skirt to the side so she's more comfortable. All she needs is a gentle movement, rub-rub, her panties on his pants, fabric on fabric. He pushes her away, his two hands out in front, the wolf flattened and the moon in quarters.

'It's not possible!' he screams, as if he was denying a terrible untruth. 'It's not possible.'

As if I've never done it, she argues. There'd be no more talk about it anymore—she can already imagine herself full of a new self-confidence, a new girl altogether, a woman, an *experienced* woman, wearing black eye shadow on her bedroom eyes.

'Don't tell me that you did it with that imbecile,' groans Bihotz. 'Don't tell me that.'

He looks so 'mystical' that she wonders if this is actually serious (is he referring to that disease where you die in two years?). In any case here's her chance not to lie to him, to be kind by telling him the truth, the whole Truth:

I'm a virgin.

The word sounds odd, pompous (Holy Mary in her tube dress with her arms raised over the church), but come on, it's the truth, technically she is *as she came from her mother's womb*, he can check if he wants to.

He looks fed up. 'You just told me you had already done it.'

I've never done it! That's what I said.

She cuddles him and he goes silent. His shaved cheeks are soft, he smells of washing powder. She rubs herself slowly on him, it feels really good. He's going to start talking again, she kisses him, she kisses his eyelids, so that, most of all, he'll keep his eyes shut, she thrusts her hips forward, she holds him tight with both arms, gripping hard, she's the Bionic Woman, he lets out a groan but the sensation is irresistible, amazing, as good as when she masturbates—when she slides her fingers near the hole and she strokes around and around, when it gets very wet—and sure enough the whole area is soaked. He can't possibly move now, watch out, she is hugging him tight and the bumps in the fabric are in just the right places and she's rubbing herself and her breasts are rubbing against the wolf, speeded-up images flash in front of her—the river and Arnaud and the Chinese screen and the disco ball and her father in the Alpine sports car—then nothing, whiteness, blankness and the whole entire world, she opens her eyes again and there's Bihotz sitting under her.

She stands up and unsticks her underpants from between her legs. This time, he looks dead. His dick is still making a pyramid shape under his overalls, a darker shape now that it's wet, right there.

It was so fast, maybe he didn't notice anything. She gives him a kiss, he opens his eyes. Would he like another beer?

She wants to be kind to him from now on. A solemn resolution: from now on she'll never say another nasty thing to him; she'll set the table and all that sort of thing; she'll never lie to him again (or only to stop him worrying); she'll make sure she only sneaks out at night when she's sleeping at her mother's house.

'It's not possible,' repeats Bihotz.

He goes out to feed the chickens, even though it's nowhere near their feed time. She can see him weeding, on his knees with his spray. He's always said it was his way to deal with stress—like that time when he had to go to the beach with her and the girls from Paris and Rose and her mother. It all seems impossibly far away, all those things they did together.

Her father takes her for a drive, in the Alpine sports car that reappears, metallic blue, in a screech of brakes in front of Bihotz's house. Bihotz is flabbergasted (no, Bihotz has now got his weeding face on). Her father takes her driving to the marina; he would have liked to take her to the sea but it's already tight time-wise. I promise, next time.

She remembers when she was little and he spoke to her about the end of all the animals. And of how Clèves would vitrify when the bombs came.

Does he want to tell her something? Like in films when they meet in a visitor's booth in prison, except a booth with scenery passing by, a gear stick and a handbrake (or like in a confessional).

'Make the most of the car, because your mother is going to make me sell it.'

She's got to say something but her mind goes blank. They're used to driving in silence. They actually get on best that way.

'Blah blah blah blah,' he adds, oddly, as if he was speaking to himself in a primitive language, the language of some desolate country with yurts and nomads. And he's shaking his head, like a yak or a camel.

She should be able to explain to him what's happening to her: that her brain stops just when she wants to speak. Like getting bogged in the snow.

As soon as she got into the Alpine, she was overwhelmed by an indescribable sensation. Azzaro for Men. Somebody must have given it to her father. The interior of the car is so choked with the fragrance it's like inhaling Arnaud straight, Arnaud's dissolved body filling her mouth, her nose, her lungs, running through her veins and pounding between her thighs.

She tries to form words with her mouth. But they burst like bubbles and she's left with a feeling of blankness, a wrinkle that smoothes out as soon as it appears, that fades as soon as she thinks it.

Perhaps that's what he's feeling himself. It's in his silence. In his cologne. It's harmony that words would destroy. They understand each other so well.

Lætitia has invited her to go over and revise maths together. She goes through the gate, rings the bell at the main entrance, and Delphine's mother opens the door: Mademoiselle is upstairs. (She must have been told that

Solange was calling in at the chateau.)

Lætitia's room is on the top floor; there are posters but also real pictures, paintings with frames. It's another blue bedroom (if, in fact, the one she was in with Arnaud was blue), the arrangement is the same: a king-size bed opposite the window, an ensuite, a balcony over the river with a view down to the swimming pool. Lætitia is lying right where Arnaud was; her little black-clad feet are pushing back the bedspread and she's snuggling up in the sheets as if she was cold.

Arnaud, Arnaud, that's her disease, she can't stop thinking about Arnaud, she's been infected and her whole brain, her body, is full of him. She's got to tell Lætitia what's going on.

I went out with Arnaud, I hope that's okay with you.

'Why wouldn't it be okay with me?'

He told me you two had something going.

'In his dreams. But it's true that we are quite close. We have the same moral standards; he has high moral standards, he's a very clean-cut guy. And very perceptive when he wants to be.'

Yes, he's a good guy.

'He's someone you can really talk to. People think it's cool to diss someone else. Well, actually it isn't; with him you can talk properly about others. Did he say stuff about me to you?'

No. And about me to you?

'All he said was that you were a bit young. But he didn't say it in a nasty way. He told me it was a bit like you were playing with yourself.'

An avalanche of snow is about to freeze her brain.

That old joke. I just unleashed my sensuality on him. That's what frightened him. When I want to be, I'm a total nympho.

'It's true that his problem is that he doesn't accept his own desires. You have to guide him. He never takes the initiative. He's like, so *phobic.*

Anyway, once you've seen his mother, you get why he's messed up.

'You know, I don't like people badmouthing others, and if I happen to have done nasty things to other people, I didn't mean to. But I really don't trust myself now...'

Why?

She'd like to keep talking about Arnaud and clear the debris from the avalanche but she has to be polite, especially on her first visit here.

'I used to be good all the time but I've got repressed feelings, buried very deep, which keep coming up—and you can't do anything about it if they overwhelm you. Take Delphine, for example, I know for a fact that she says horrible things about me, but she's just too much, and I'm no Good Samaritan.'

The truth is she's a hick.

'You can't say that, it's not like it's her fault. But she is really annoying. I can't tell her, and I never would tell her anyway, but she's self-centred. And she's got a big head.'

Exactly. She thinks she's so great, it's crazy.

'It's normal for her to talk about herself, and she does it endlessly, as if she's the only person in the whole world. She can't see beyond her own navel.'

According to Lætitia, Delphine is very sensitive, and that explains everything.

She's a megalomaniac, adds Solange.

'Megalomaniac?'

Yes, she's always going on about her father who died or whatever and her working-class mother.

'Domestic servant,' corrects Lætitia. 'Delphine is like my sister. My parents had a daughter before me and she died, Blue Disease. I think about her all the time, I imagine being buried underground and I say to myself: why is she rotting with the worms and my heart is still beating?'

Lætitia looks exceptionally beautiful when she utters these words, the extraordinary Blue Disease seems to be flowing in her veins; it's obvious now why she always wears black. She's smoking, and frowning.

What was her name?

'Lætitia.'

Lætitia the same as you?

'Lætitia d'Urbide. It's my mother's favourite first name.'

Veins in the shape of L and U pulse on her pale forehead. She reaches her arm towards the ashtray but the table is too far away and she tips back into the cushions as if it was too much effort, and that's exactly what Solange wants—that style and that elegance—she tips back too, onto the pouffe, and sighs.

It's really fantastic. You and I have so many things in common, as well as Arnaud. We understand each other so *well.*

Delphine's mother brings in a tray with glasses and Coca-Cola. 'Straws,' demands Lætitia. They wait in silence for her return with the straws.

Lætitia is wearing a pencil skirt, patent leather court shoes that she flips on and off, a little black jacket that she removes because it's hot, and a sort of body stocking in black lace, transparent across the shoulders and opaque across her breasts, with long gauze sleeves.

'The difference between being girlfriends and being friends,' Lætitia continues, 'is that girlfriends get on really well together, whereas true friendship is stronger but potentially more destructive.'

That doesn't frighten me. I can be really intense when I want to be.

'Are you still friends with Rose?'

She hasn't changed at all and I have a lot. She's a nerd, she doesn't smoke dope, doesn't take drugs or do anything.

'There are things she just couldn't understand. She is too...not intense enough. I have to think of my own interests and it's something I just can't accept.'

I so agree with you. She's become frivolous, trivial. She's got a Ciao, it's the same as a moped but better.

'I know. It's frivolous, trivial.'

She's a girl who doesn't have the courage to be humble, to ask others for help. I've got too much self-respect to put up with that. I have to do what's right for me.

'She doesn't know how to be in the background. She's got too much personality. When you think about it, it's just unrestrained personality. She always has to be the centre of attention. I'm hypersensitive. My mother's always telling me. I could have ended up with a big personality too, but thanks to the fact that I'm hypersensitive, I think about other people.'

I so agree. At least you aren't conventional. You've avoided all that image stuff. Not like Arnaud.

'Yes. But sometimes not doing things like others gets to be so common it becomes conventional. Do you see what I mean? I imagine myself as I imagine others imagine me and I do the opposite. I don't try to be different, I just am, because to be like others think you are, or to want to be like you think they think you are, is straight-out frivolous, trivial.'

For sure.

Lætitia is gesturing with her long gauzy arms in front of her face, and her bouffant hair smells incredibly good—expensive shampoo, expensive air held inside the puffy mass of hair.

'My problem is that I'm so perceptive. The fact that I know where I am means I'm terribly lost. Because where I am is not pretty at all.' As she says this, Lætitia seems to be on the edge of tears.

How could it be possible not to be happy with your lot in a chateau with a pool—

Why?

'I know perfectly well, I have one failing: I'm perceptive.'

Lætitia seems suddenly distraught, leaning back in the cushions. She should *console* her (for what?), pat her soufflé of chestnut hair, or try to distract her, put a pillow on her head and pretend to be Napoleon like Jacques Dutronc in *The Most Important Thing: Love* that she secretly watched on TV without Bihotz knowing.

She leans towards the hair that is still as fluffy as ever and buries her nose in it, there is no end to this marvellous cloud of hair.

Lætitia lowers her eyes to her straw. A thin black streak outlines the length of her eyelids (how does she manage not to go over the edges?). Her face is right up close, large and flat like an object. Then it comes alive and turns towards Solange; the eyes open and the gaze radiant; Lætitia, Lætitia's mouth finds her mouth.

She leans in from her side, the taste is sparkling fresh, her elbow slides, their teeth smash, the Coke glasses clink together—they both pull back.

(Is Lætitia a *lesbian*?)

(At one point in *The Most Important Thing: Love* you see a woman who is disguised as a man with an actual false dick tied on with a sort of harness, and a completely naked girl who looks mad or on drugs, and we're supposed to interpret that, well, the whole thing seems impossible but it's nevertheless strongly hinted at.)

She has to say something.

(Does Lætitia have hairs on her breasts?)

That's the first time I've done it with a girl.

Which makes it clear that, on the other hand, she's done it with boys.

'Me too,' whispers Lætitia.

It'll be our secret. We won't tell anyone. Promise me? Promise.

'I promise,' says Lætitia solemnly. She shakes her legs and wiggles her hips to rearrange her clothes.

We won't tell anyone but I'm happy if we talk about it together.

Lætitia lights a cigarette and doesn't say anything.

I mean I'm happy if we talk about it, so that we don't end up embarrassed or whatever—as if that could even be embarrassing, and as if we'd never talk about it.

It feels like she's split in half and she can see herself talking, serious and apprehensive, sitting on the edge of the bed with Solange and Lætitia—where's the first Lætitia gone, the one who wanted to kiss her?

I'm sure we'll remember this moment for the rest of our lives, she perseveres. *The rest of our lives. I'm absolutely certain.*

Lætitia is also absolutely certain. With the tips of her fingernails she plays with a ladder in her stay-up stockings. On the other hand (says the young baroness), it's not as if you can *decide* what you'll remember; she manages to forget far more important things, and also to have moments when she's struck by the certainty that what she (Lætitia) is experiencing right then she will remember forever, and yet afterwards she forgets. Or else, oddly, she remembers tiny details. For example, a flash of landscape out of the window of the Audi, something completely outside herself and which, God knows why, is imprinted on her memory forever. At the time it seems like nothing at all, and in fact it's an intense moment embedded in her brain like, she doesn't know, a diamond.

Solange agrees completely.

That leaves them both musing.

Apparently Delphine is a *nympho.* Not exactly a whore or a slut. Nor a *loose girl.* She's more verging on the pathological side (explains Nathalie). That means she can't help herself, not to harm anyone but simply because she can't think of anything else. Even worse than Slurp. And she's itching to do it so much that she does it with anyone. She's even dyed her hair purple. She's deflowered half the boys at school, apparently. Including Arnaud, apparently (and recently).

And she's the daughter of a single mother.

'I don't see the connection,' Rose interrupts.

For a few months now Rose has been making threatening comments in a super-responsible tone but with a really open mind. Like her parents. She'd probably get on well with Lætitia (except they can't stand each other).

'If her mother had had the right to have an abortion'—Rose continues—'Delphine wouldn't even be here to be called a nympho.'

Concepción makes the sign of the cross discreetly.

(Apparently if you make the sign of the cross upside down you go to Hell.)

'Do you think it was out of pleasure'—Rose is adamant—'that her mother fell pregnant at our age?'

A world without Delphine. In that world, she's certain that she, Solange, would be the one doing what Delphine's doing. Sleeping with all the boys. Not in a superior, stylish way like Lætitia, or cool and liberated like Nathalie, but in a grubby I-can't-help-myself way. That's her problem. She's a nympho. That's her disease.

The others (Rose, Nathalie, Concepción) have got their heads bent over their history-geography books. They're all at Concé's for a study session. The Yalta Agreement. There are only men in the photo.

Is she really the only one to be seeing this—only seeing dicks under those thick overcoats? All those dicks surrounded by pubic hair (brown, blond, grey, white), flopped onto the bellies of those seated men, hanging in the boxer shorts of the ones standing behind? The crotch is all creased on the one in the middle, the only one whose pants you can see. Can you really manage to concentrate when you have a dick? Weren't they thinking about their dicks when they were signing those agreements? Wouldn't their dicks have started going hard *inadvertently* right when they were in the middle of dividing up the world? Dicks living their dick lives in all those pairs of pants, little gnome dicks on each of those men, dicks doing their dick business. The Yalta dicks, washed or unwashed, limp or erect, stinky or clean-smelling, chafing or still, dicks that no one bothers about or, on the contrary, dicks that are the focus of each of those men's thoughts.

That's what she wants to learn, the History of the Dick, what you do and how you live when you have that instead of this.

She tips back and forth on the hard wood of her chair, the seam of her jeans gently rubs the flesh between her legs, she wiggles her hips discreetly. Solange has an *unbridled sensuality*.

This afternoon of history-geography is so boring (she's got to stop using *so*). She'll get them to focus on her. Make it all a bit more exciting, this scene, those heads bent over those books, those fannies stuck on those chairs.

Lætitia wanted to sleep with me.

An atomic bomb. Nathalie looks so stunned, it was worth it just to see that. Rose giggles and Concepción crosses herself again, it's a tic, like some people twist their hair or bite their fingernails or say 'Oh my God'. Nathalie and Rose want all the details, of course (Concé as well, even though she stays mute).

She asked me when I went to see her at the chateau.

She waits for a moment. For effect, but also because

she's hesitating. What should she tell them? What's the best thing to tell them?

She made out with me, it was divine, better than with all the boys I've kissed.

Nathalie's mouth is wide open, her eyes are rolling and she topples off her chair and falls on the ground, miming groans of agony.

Seriously, only girls know how to kiss. When I think how we waste our time with boys.

Rose decides to be *self-possessed.* While Nathalie is yelping on the carpet demanding to know, did you smoke or what, she says that when she, Rose, did it with girls, it was not quite as good as with boys. Because, come on, there's penetration. You can say what you like.

But what sort of a moron are you, of course she wanted to penetrate *me, I was the one who didn't want it. I'm not going to let myself be raped by a dyke.*

Lætitia had a sort of plastic dick that she wanted to put in Solange's bottom, well, in her cunt.

Concepción has her hand over her mouth.

'There's no such thing as a plastic dick,' Nathalie declares.

Yes there is, you tie it on around your waist, like this.

'Yeah, right. Stop talking bullshit.'

As usual, when the conversation gets serious, Rose launches into a speech with several points she wants to make, like how, firstly, her mother actually has a plastic dick too,

Rose found it in the drawer of her bedside table; and that, secondly, it's not right to make fun of dykes, firstly (thirdly) it's a rude word, and that, fourthly, everyone does what they want, we live in a democracy, after all we're in France under a socialist president.

('My parents voted for Mitterand to help people like you,' she told Solange when half the village wanted to flee the country. 'Personally, I would have voted Workers' Struggle. The socialists are hypocrites; at the end of the day they're just helping big business.' She seemed so intelligent, mature, *sexy*, when she said that. It's horrible that Rose's vote is charity for Solange's parents who are being *screwed* by voting for the right.)

'It's cool to be *bisexual*,' chimes in Nathalie belatedly (she is now wearing her Super-Nathalie costume). 'Anyway, everyone is bisexual. Boys are bisexual too.'

Protests all round.

'Bisexual means two girls at the same time,' explains Nathalie.

Concepción confirms this: her female cousin from Saragossa did it with her girlfriend's boyfriend *and* her girlfriend. 'The girlfriend was getting laid and my cousin gave him blowjob.'

Gave him A blowjob, corrects Solange. *It's like Jane Birkin saying she'll sing 'UN chanson' instead of 'UNE chanson' when she's been living in France for two hundred years.*

'But was there only one penis?' Rose says, surprised.

Her rapid logic—or her practical mind—makes everyone laugh (or maybe it was the word penis).

'Do you know how you say vagina in Spanish?' says Nathalie. '*Esclusa*, a canal lock. Because that's where the peniche boats go through, get it—penis-peniche.'

Concé is too engrossed in the conversation to be insulted (or to understand).

Did the boy take it in turns? A go in the mouth, a go in the cunt? Everything seems possible.

Her three friends focus on the incident, which has captured their imaginations, mesmerised them. In the centre of the room their bodies vanish, leaving behind their schoolgirl shells. They look like the pale children in *The Village of the Damned*.

'He was forty,' Concepción explains. 'The girlfriend's boyfriend.'

It all adds up. But the images flickering there—naked bodies in the trembling space—are still tricky to hold steady in their minds, a bit like stubborn Playmobil pieces, they don't fit into what the girls have glimpsed of the world so far: a certain elasticity that is attractive, disturbing—or perhaps (Solange's great fear) just as limited as Clèves.

Concepción goes and finds her mother's shopping catalogue, *Trois Chuiches*. She flips through the lingerie pages. It's not there. They grab the catalogue from her. You have to look in the bathroom section, feminine health and hygiene and all that. Between breast pumps, shower caps and back-scratchers, there is a portable face massager—in an odd, pointed shape—that firms features and smoothes out nasolabial folds. Home delivery with two batteries.

'That's it!' exclaims Rose. 'See, I'm not making it up.' It's like she's completely forgotten that she, Solange, was raped by Lætitia.

A little shrapnel shell, longer than it is wide, like a suppository but bigger. The girl in the photo, some bimbo in white cotton, is holding it against her cheek, looking like she's just seen the Virgin Mary. She looks like her. She's struck by it. The same angle of the head, the same melancholic gaze, the same blank stare as in the photo of her when she was five or six. Against her cheek she's holding the cloth nappy that used to be her security blanket. So soft and fluffy, it was as light as a feather: a scrap of towelling, a relic from an extinct species.

'Is that what d'Urbide wanted to put inside you?' Concepción is checking to make sure.

Suddenly she feels very tired. She's been tied down or drugged, like the young girl in *The Most Important Thing: Love*. Lætitia—an older Lætitia, or perhaps Rose's mother (with her red boots)—is leaning above her (or behind her?) (she's on all fours?) and is going to *put it in, put it in her*. She'd like to be in her bed, falling asleep with her hand in her underpants. She's sick. She must be sick.

'She's just a big dyke.' Nathalie winds up the conversation despite calls for *tolerance* from Rose. 'A dirty fucking lesbian, carrying on like butter wouldn't melt in her mouth.'

'Arnaud calls her Cheap Carpet.' Concepción bursts out laughing. (Concepción *knows* Arnaud?)

(She's sliding on the surface of a planet that is spinning too fast. In the end, the only thing that is certain, the only thing to hold on to [besides the ballast of the dead, but that weight doesn't count] is the fleshy mass of the creature between her legs, alive and thick, pulsing, getting hairier and more and more autonomous, huge, intense, unknown, opening its moist, puckered and discerning maw to gobble up the history-geography textbook.)

(If she hangs back, frightened, studying in a bedroom with her wretched lifelong girlfriends, this creature will end up breaking away from her, crawling out on its belly with those hairy legs, hungry to devour the world. It will end up running around by itself, living its voracious bestial life, and return home to the den between her legs, to make her come, alone and miserable in her bed.)

'I don't want to hurt you,' Arnaud says to her on the phone. 'You absolutely mustn't fall in love with me, that's the worst thing that could happen to you, monogamy just isn't my thing, life's too short to be monogamous—what musician only plays one scale? Ah, my little Angie, you're sweet, you're good enough to eat, but the thing is you have to think of yourself, I'm about to leave for Bordeaux, didn't

I tell you? I got into Philosophy, you should come and visit me, but my girlfriend might get angry, there's no way you can stay with me at the uni dorm, I'll come and visit you in your village, in your little village, in your bedroom with your dolls, I've got a feeling that will turn me on big time, what, you don't have dolls anymore? I'm joking, I've got a car now, I'll come by and pick you up, and you'll do things to me that I like, you know, with your tongue, you don't do it as well as my girlfriend but you get much more turned on, I adore how you let yourself go, do you like letting yourself go? You're a bit masochistic, I adore that. What are you wearing right now? Tell me what you're wearing. You mustn't wait for me, find yourself someone good, a reliable guy, a *big bloke* from your village. Kiss me, kiss me better, on the cock, come on, on my dick okay, I'm holding it hard here, go on suck me, quickly, I've gotta hang up, touch your breasts, touch yourself I'm telling you, put your finger in your arsehole—Ar Ar Arnooooo—go on, yes, go on, I've gotta hang up, think about me and wiggle your little arse, bitch oh oh—Arnoooooooo—think of me in your little arse Ar Ar…'

'That guy's pretty classy.' Nathalie is impressed when she tells her about the rather unexpected phone call—his first phone call, the first time he's called her off his *own bat*—that he even thought of calling her before he left for Bordeaux, already at uni, already *in a relationship*—a phone call that made her so happy and left her consumed with desire and filled with questions. 'He's right about monogamy, you can't really expect a guy like that to stay celibate, come back to earth, my girl, you have to be more liberated, but doing it on the phone must be really really exciting, I'm not kidding, I'm so jealous.'

She ignored the bit about being masochistic, she didn't really understand it anyway and also the bit about her finger in her arsehole, that's a bit embarrassing (even though she normally tells Nathalie everything). In the end, when she thinks about it, maybe she is a little bit uptight.

Her mother gets dressed to go out, in her Liberty-print harem-pants jumpsuit. Won't Solange put hers on too? They have a job to do. Both of them. Women's business. It's important. Solange is old enough to understand now. It feels like they're wearing flowers to go and kill someone.

It's one of the mornings when the shop is shut, when it seems like her mother has some scores to settle. She doesn't have her customers to deal with, and it's like she's on the wrong setting, as if she wanted to persuade Solange to buy the stock from her—she's using proper grammar and a northern accent, Parisian, a threatening accent, her shop accent.

It's the first of November, All Saints Day, but it's as hot as a summer's day. The sky is deep blue. The plane trees have red leaves. The American oaks are an overstated red (everything is overstated in America). It's like a trick of the light: the sharply defined lobes on the leaves, embossed by the scorching wind. And she feels excluded from the scenery, as if the world was inaccessible to her beneath its froth of colours.

Her mother has bought huge pots of flowers to match the trees. Red, brown and golden. Every year Solange sees these pots in the garage. They rattle around in the back of the Renault 5. Papa's Alpine wasn't in the garage. It wasn't in front of the pharmacy either (you never know).

They go past the Cheap Carpet outlet and Milord's and the silos. They even go past the marina, but they don't take the road to the sea. They drive through all the vineyards on the d'Urbide estate. After that there are still kilometres of corn.

'Corn is so ugly. Right at eye level like that. At least wheat can wave. And the sea has a horizon. But because of your father, we had to be next to the airport. Trapped in corn country. We're not chickens!' Her mother clucks, hoping to make her laugh.

All of a sudden they go downhill, and it's the beginning of another country, on another contour line, as if her mother had found the entrance to another dimension, science-fiction style. It's a land of pine trees, with sand dunes. She listens distractedly while her mother explains to her that this forest was planted by hand. Every now and then a yellow clearing appears, with heather and red ferns, and it's like witnessing a moment without mankind, a glimpse into an earlier time: seeing the earth pared of all thought, of any human gaze. She breathes deeply through her mouth, trying to get in touch with this, with Nature from a time before *homo sapiens*. As soon as she sees a clearing, she concentrates and it passes into her body, matter from the beginning, the original atoms.

'Do you want me to stop? Are you feeling sick?'

She'd like to go to America. In America there must be heaps of places where no man (or woman) has ever set foot (have ever set feet). Actually, her head's spinning (or puffed-up) from trying to think about the Earth without human beings. And about the atoms of dead Indians, who were themselves made out of dinosaur atoms carried by the wind and the sea, and from which she herself is constituted at this very moment as she breathes in.

Her mother parks in front of a stone wall and greets an old woman who has a lot of watering-cans. 'I'd like you to meet my daughter, Solange.' Hello to the lady, whose atoms look authentically old. 'I was just saying to myself that I knew you would come,' said the lady. 'You've never missed a year. And your husband? Men, always working. All Saints Day, and already we're seeing buds on the pine trees.'

It's a small cemetery with lopsided graves that are not so much covered in soil as silted up. Her mother, in the harem jumpsuit, has loaded herself up with flower pots and given Solange a watering-can to fill at the tap over there. There are graves with the date 1857 and 1864 and even 1893, the year they chopped off Marie Antoinette's head. Amazing she can remember anything from her boring history classes.

There's no border between the sand she's treading on and the sand covering the dead bodies. Nothing but a little gravel to bear the weight of the living as they walk past. If not for that she'd sink right down into the graves, or a hand would reach out from the sand, like in *Carrie*, and grab her by the ankle. The gravel keeps her above the abyss, just like circles of ashes keep vampires at bay.

'Solange?'

Her mother. She gets started with the watering-can, the tap sticks, hurry up. The old woman's shadow is laughing on the wall. She runs across to her mother, spilling water as she goes, jumping over the glass caskets of the immortals, the ceramic flowers, the angels in faded shades and the In Memoriams in flaky engraving. She mustn't walk on the graves. Walk *between* the graves.

Her head is buried in her mother's harem jumpsuit and everything has shrunk: they're miniature tombs now. Her mother is tending the dead, digging over the sand, planting things, pulling out weeds and knotted grass, gauzy strands, tangled bits and pieces that she replants and buries. She unpots the big flowers, telling Solange to water them as she digs them into the soil, jabbing her nails in. When her mother rinses her hands under the tap, the water sweeps her sweat, cells, atoms into the sand where they can regenerate, intermingled with the dead of this place.

The photo in the seal on the tombstone is the same as the one on her mother's bedside table. Now that she tries to think about it again in the car, she's getting the photo confused with the one she sees everywhere, in the newspapers and on the TV, of the little boy who was thrown into the river and whose name is Grégory, Little Grégory.

On the tombstone, the date—those hypnotic numbers—show that he died before her date of birth. A bit later and it would have been the date of her birthday engraved on the stone, which makes no sense at all, except if, like two ships passing in the night, she and her parents' son had just missed each other.

There must have been a first name, but at night in her bed it's no use leaving the light on and trying to visualise the tomb again, the image just fades, the car moves off and the cornfields grow back, along with the vineyards and Milord's and the Cheap Carpet outlet, while the grave and the first name remain back there, as well as the sand and the roots of the plants, and the flowerpots. It was back there and she's forgotten (and asking would mean puncturing a hole in that country back there so it can pour into this country, the only even vaguely liveable one, the only one even vaguely possible).

At last, the sea.

They were dozing in his van after their swim, he was stroking her arms, her knees, her hips, and now he's got his head on her thighs, his mouth grazing the hem of her swimsuit, it's almost unbearable.

It's like the thing she's got between her legs is clamouring for something to drink, without worrying about her head, up there, which is not *so* thirsty, or which, let's say, is just observing the thirsty thing down there. (She's got to stop the whole *so* thing.)

There must come a time, when you're an adult, when you do everything automatically—that thing and all the rest—when you're relaxed, not having to *feel* everything like this. (Solange is so sensitive.)

She takes his hand and puts it there, where it's thirsty. All the water in her body streams down there into her swimsuit that's already wet from the sea. If only he'd put his fingers inside, a few fingers. But he's just touching the elastic gently and almost tenderly. So she squeezes his big head between her legs and rubs against him as best she can, on his nose, on his forehead, on his mouth, on whatever bit is sticking out. She writhes around to make him move where she wants him, oh my God, if only he'd stick his tongue in a bit—but he doesn't want to. She presses like mad but he stays on the surface, so tactful, so scrupulous she could scream.

'I'm going mad.' Bihotz sits up (whereas she's the one who's going mad).

'I'm going mad,' he repeats, pleading almost, as if he was begging for help from the seagulls.

He's moved into the front seat. His upper lip is

glistening, as if he's drunk a beer. Just looking at that lip makes her squirm, her frustration unassuaged.

She remembers that it's got a Latin name, since it's a bit gynaecological and they didn't find a good simple word like 'head job'. The only time someone ever talked about it with her was when Nathalie said real men don't do it. That it's a gay thing. There's no way Arnaud would ever do a thing like that.

It's not like she can *jerk off* right now. She slides in next to him and in the same movement pulls up the bottom of her swimsuit. Nothing can happen in the front seat. It's a molten world behind the windscreen. They're in an aquarium where liquid sun has replaced the water. The sea and the sun are exploding. Rocks, the boom of the surf, colours, and the screech of the seagulls in bursts of red.

She finally got her day at the sea. She frightened him when she swam in the surf, not wanting to get out. She asked for ice-creams. Then she didn't want to go back to Clèves and they went to a restaurant. She scarcely touched her prawns but she devoured her chocolate fondant. She felt a bit sick so they lay in the back of his van before leaving, the sunset blazing through the windscreen.

Now he's looking at her, right through her, as if he could see Death or something.

Stop sulking.

The way he's sitting makes wrinkles in the tattoos on his naked torso. The tiger has grown a long snout. The rose has slanting eyes. Not much further down, under his nylon shorts, his dick is doing its pyramid thing. He's like a man made out of different parts, plus the skull and the band's name AC/DC on his arm. Apparently that means *Anti-Christ* or something.

A few metres in front of them, surfers are doing impossible manoeuvres. The spray separating them from the surfers is like the line between the living and the dead—but it suddenly occurs to her that perhaps she's the one who's alive, *perhaps I'm alive and all the others are dead* (except Bihotz, who is somewhat encumbered by his conspicuous body).

Camping on the beach where they are parked is a group of people they will never connect with. Because she and Bihotz are wretched Clèvians, pathetic villagers, isolated forever. These surfers are sliding around in the centre of a world that is turning without her. Their eyes see only the waves, their ears hear only the call of mermaids, their radar wouldn't even pick up her presence. These surfers are not of this world; they're not mere flesh and blood, and as for their dicks, do they even have dicks?

A guy from the van next to them is hanging his wetsuit on a washing line. He's really blond, sea-blue eyes, a sun-burnished nose, a joint hanging from his chapped lips.

Behind the rocks, waves are breaking, ghosts rising out of the blue, arms in all directions, crashing down, flooded with red light.

The guy with the peeling lips is kissing a female creature.

Like Venus on her scallop shell, she seems to have emerged just like that in her fluoro string bikini. A moist mouth, soothing hands—she was put on earth to moisturise him all over. (She recalls an ad from when she was little: a semi-naked girl announcing, 'Tomorrow I'm taking off my pants.')

Bihotz turns on the van's ignition and reverses. They drive back without speaking. Their silence is like an elastic band that stretches from where they were, by the sea, and extends, taut to the point of snapping, all the way to Clèves.

Her mother asks her to mind the shop as she has to see a *lawyer.* It's Saturday but the village is empty. The south wind has scattered everyone off to the seaside. Standing behind the shop window, she's filled again with that searing sensation of everything that's missing here.

She still took care with her outfit: a pair of 501 jeans passed on from Lætitia (and accepted gratefully), a loose-knit cotton top that flatters her small boobs, and a bandana knotted across her forehead, with a bouffant hairdo on top. She checks herself out in the squares of mirror stuck on the wall drapes (for clients who want to see what they look like when they try on the knitted vests). It's great how much taller a pair of 501s can make you look.

23 57 01

Not a single phone call from Arnaud since he's been in Bordeaux.

The telephone is sitting there, horribly accessible, like a chocolate pudding with the spoon already in it. But does he even have a phone in his uni dorm?

Ding, dong, bell,

Pussy's in the well.

Who put her in?

Who pulled her out?

Bihotz of course. Exactly like he's always predicted.

She wanders around barefoot like Catherine Deneuve in *Le Sauvage*. When she lights all the candle jars, as her mother instructed her to, everything gets hotter and shimmers red-orange.

The Key to Clèves, a name chosen by the previous owner, who already sold Virgin Mary barometers and pewter platters. An interior décor boutique, not a souvenir shop, insists her mother. (And definitely not a store. But why not a supermarket like the Kudeshayans run?)

And yet the same things have been here forever. Souvenirs waiting to find a home. Waiting to be forgotten under the dust, to become invisible after being there so long. But they'll outlive their purchasers just like the soft toy dogs outlived Madame Bihotz. Souvenirs in the shape of crystal dolphins, enamelled metal owls, porcelain ringed hands, *Doctor Zhivago* musical boxes, princesses made out of shells, snow domes with distressed figures inside, their outlines blurred, their arms raised in the blizzard.

Above all, there is the *box of secrets*—it's been written

there on top since Solange learned to read. A little chest with labelled drawers: *my birth bracelet*, *my first lock of hair*, *my first dummy*, *my first tooth*, and even *my first movie ticket*, everything organised chronologically in cute compartments. She has always coveted this object. It's expensive, 199 francs. Time is passing, everyone's time, Clèves' time. Soon it will be too late. *My first wedding ring*, she daydreams. *(My first Tampax.)*

Her mother makes a point of dusting it, she's frightened it will go out of fashion.

The shop window is a rectangle of dusty sunlight, framing a view of the village with drifting shadows.

Ding a ling—Rose and her mother.

Her back straightens instantly, an orthopaedic-commercial reflex inherited from her mother (and her father). (Two parents, two *whores*.)

Rose's mother's red boots tap on the tiled floor. (Apparently she is leading a double life, on the coast.) They greet each other with a kiss.

They are looking for a present for Rose's father. A Rubik's Cube. They're allowed a five per cent discount with their loyalty card. She wraps it up nicely, tugging on the gift ribbon with the edge of the scissors. Gift ribbon is something Rose knows nothing about. Rose's mother is in raptures at how the pretty flowers of ribbon curl up like that.

Rose, who reads *Best* magazine, tells her that Marvin Gaye has been killed by his own father. Rose's mother says she should come round and listen to the record at home, it's so stupid, these two young girls don't see each other any more: her witness is Madame Kudeshayan, who has just come into the shop, *ding a ling*, followed by her son and Raphaël Bidegarraï, *ding a ling ding a ling*, it's getting crowded.

There's a staggering family resemblance between all these Clèveans, an actual *familiarity* about them. Even though Madame Kudeshayan is as black as (if Solange remembers correctly) Marvin Gaye was. It's quite surprising in an Indian woman (or Pakistani, or whatever she is). She would have expected beige-coloured, or dark salmon-pink. And her son's skin colour is not much lighter (nor her husband's).

It must be the village. It's changed. It's become a city. It seems like even the Kudeshayans have become diluted. Perhaps the efforts of Rose's parents have finally borne fruit—they swapped their Solidarity union badges for the yellow hands logo of SOS Racism. (*You should sell those hands*, Solange told her mother.)

For example, you can't even tell anymore that Concepción is Spanish; she even wants to call herself Magali. And apparently Bihotz's father was Jewish. But if anyone can testify that Bihotz's dick hasn't been cut, it's her. And her mother explained that you can't be Jewish and also have a name from around here. She would really like to ask her father to confirm this point but he seems to have completely done a runner. Yes, perhaps Clèves is becoming a modern village, an American *melting pot*, a *mixed* village like the cheese, *fromage mixe*, because people are all the same anyway and racism is really dumb.

'You really are becoming more and more of a babe.'

Raphaël Bidegarraï's acne has got worse, it's as if the diaeresis in his name has spread all over his skin. There are rumours—incredible—that he might be with Rose. (Poor Christian.)

Meanwhile the two mothers (Rose's and the Kudeshayan mother) are still chatting away, as if they were at home, and all for a thirty-nine-franc Rubik's Cube. And the Kudeshayan (Cutie Shitting) kid is fiddling with the trinkets—and, she can't believe it, he's turning his nose up at them.

YOU BREAK, YOU PAY. She wants to wave the sign under his nose. She can almost understand why her mother gets migraines.

'Clèves—how could you leave.' The sign had finally been erected at the entrance to the village, after consultation with Clèveans of voting age. 'Achieve at Clèves' was thought to be too much of an *advertisement*. And Rose's mother was against the line 'Believe in Clèves' (false advertising, in her opinion). Madame Kudeshayan had laughed: 'Anyway, it won't be long before the independence movement start to graffiti the sign with their mumbo jumbo.'

If she could vote (but who cares about teenagers?) she'd like 'Clèves, cleave to me'. Clèves actually does make you think of clinging to somebody. And it starts with the same letters as clitoris.

'That d'Urbide bitch is a fat dyke,' Bidegarraï whispers to her. 'Arnaud Lemoine wanted to fuck her and she yelled that it was rape and told him that she only did it with girls.'

You're kidding?

(Arnaud and Lætitia. That rumour, of course.)

'She was having sex with Delphine. She got up in the middle of the night to eat her out—all she had to do was go downstairs.' A pimple of excitement explodes on his forehead. 'And Delphine, no surprises there. The only thing she hasn't lain down for is a train, oh and girls, trains and girls...'

He's trying to be witty but he's lost the thread. She cuts in: *She even got laid by Cheap Carpet.*

Their laughter catches the attention of the two mothers. Apparently Delphine is getting better, they feared the worst, but she only took about ten sleeping pills. Her mother had left them lying around, how mindless, what a messed-up family. The women lower their voices.

'She even got laid by Cheap Carpet,' Bidegarraï echoes in her ear, stifling a burst of laughter.

He's really overdoing it now. Bidegarraï, the guy who held her head under the tap, the guy who cornered her in the playground, the guy who stuck his hands on her breasts when they were what, ten, Bidegarraï who's ugly now and covered in acne, that Bidegarraï is now looking for her approval. Has he forgotten everything? (Nathalie is always telling her that with boys, everything comes back to their dicks. 'With most boys anyway,' she adds.) He smells of Azzaro for Men but the whole world has started to smell of Azzaro.

And how can she make the word *dyke* fit in with that moment in Lætitia's bedroom—a moment like the light from the candle jars, shimmering and hot, a moment she likes to recall, rekindle, even though neither of them has uttered a single word about it—not that they're embarrassed, no, but they just behave as if nothing happened.

'It's a lamp made out of salt from the Himalayas,' the Kudeshayan mother is explaining to her son (the Himalayas, my arse). She's holding the lamp in her cupped hands and she tells him to put the tip of his tongue on the lamp.

Instead of stopping them, Solange lets them carry on. She's mesmerised. It's as if the mother was recalling memories of her times in the mountains, of paths among the glaciers, and with the tip of his tongue, her son, a loving son, was tasting the salt with a gesture both dutiful and playful. A loving son, yet another find in this curiosity shop—a mother and son laughing together over a little lamp, able to share the world, its continents, its exploration, its riches. Such exotic items, a lamp and a loving son.

'What have you done with your key?' asks Bihotz.

Her house (her parents' house, or should she say from now on, her mother's house?) is locked. She has inflatable parents, just like those dolls. You pull out the plug and they float away, looping through the sky.

'Ever since my mother died,' says Bihotz, who's using his 'mystical' voice again, 'everything's gone wrong. We don't know who lives where anymore. This arrangement, this sharing of roles, it's confusing. I'm even starting to wonder if Lulu is really a dog.'

Lulu is dying and her scruffy muzzle seems to be inhabited by an insane number of faces: Madame Bihotz and Solange's parents and Arnaud and Lætitia and Little Gregory and the other child under the tombstone and the old woman at the cemetery and Bihotz's weight-watching fat cousin—the dead and the living and the half-dead all mixed together, or as if they were all dead, and it makes Solange want to cry.

She brushes her teeth and puts on her Snoopy night-dress. *Raiders of the Lost Ark* is on TV. The film is terrifying and she buries her head in his shoulder.

'Don't touch me,' he growls.

Such an overreaction when right in front of her eyes is the distinctive transformation of his fly into the pyramid shape. It's even more accentuated when she puts her hand on top of his (he pushes it away). It occurs to her to do what Arnaud is always asking her to do, but something doesn't seem right—her *sucking off* Bihotz, or Bihotz letting himself be—no, it's really not on.

What to do? What is a girl supposed to do?

She sticks her small breasts against his biceps just as a

bridge of vines breaks under Indiana Jones's weight. Warmth floods her chest and her heart is aching, filled with all sorts of hidden things, like in the temples, tombs and sarcophagi of *Raiders of the Lost Ark.* (But who would ever understand?)

'I hope you went to visit Delphine in hospital?' grumbles Bihotz.

He visited her poor mother, who can't get over it. But it was nothing, right? An adolescent fling, and she just reacted without thinking—fancy doing that to her mother! She wraps her leg around his thigh. She'd like him to take her in his arms, right there, *shhh,* she'd like some rest and for it all to stop and for something (what?) to pick her up and carry her away without her having to do a thing—then she'd be ready and willing for anything.

'Anyway, Solange, you don't like anyone, you have a heart of stone, that's the truth.'

Bihotz gets up. He's got his pharaoh silhouette, the profile of the pyramid sticking out from his dressing-gown. It's so pathetic how visible *nymphomania* is in men.

'Your parents' marriage is about to disintegrate and you're just enjoying yourself, Mademoiselle thinks she's at a hotel, Mademoiselle just wants to have her nails done, Mademoiselle thinks everyone is there to serve her.'

It's so unfair that she bursts into tears. She's never worn nail polish in her life. It's all such a mess. After all the work she's done in the shop today, after everything she does for others, to help maintain the shop, the display, *appearances,* after everything she *gives*, her generosity, that total gift of herself, her absence of pride, when she thinks of how young she is, her *innocence* that's been *trampled on*—tears well up from deep inside her, from way down, she can't bear it anymore, she's suffocating, she's going to kill herself if that's what it's all about, it's so horribly, atrociously unfair!

'My darling, my love, my Solange, my only angel.' So now he's trying to console her. Serves him right. 'My Solange, my sunshine.' So he's kissing her on her eyes on her chin on her lips, he's wrapping his arms around her, his whole body is around her. She gives into it. She stops crying a bit. She starts to rock herself backwards and forwards on him, it feels good, she starts to work a bit harder at it, she sticks what she's got down there against what he's got down there, it's burning, it's melting, like rubbing sticks together, like molten wax, images appear in her mind (Arnaud, Indiana Jones, the Kudeshayan boy, Lætitia d'Urbide, the surfer with chapped lips), clothing and flesh part, it's a bit hard at first, she rocks forwards and repositions herself, See Saw Marjorie Daw—and something—*boing*—pops in place like a spring.

She's not crying anymore, she's concentrating very hard. She's sighing and panting. She's riding up and down, sitting squarely on his thighs, like on a horse but still not quite like that. He's kissing her *passionately*, she turns her head away and shuts her eyes but his mouth follows her, wet and gulping—*shhh!*—she sits up straight but not too straight, so the thing doesn't slip out, so that she's right up close, right there, so it rubs, when she goes down again she goes down hard, that's it, that's good, he mustn't move at all, she goes up and down but rocks backwards and forwards as well—she's got her whole life in front of her, her whole life to learn, to feel, her whole life to keep doing it.

Bihotz starts mewling like a cat and something incredibly wet and sticky spills out and he wants to take his thing out but that is absolutely not going to happen, she's much stronger than he is, she holds on to him and moves up and down and rubs at the top the bottom in front at the back and keeps going and weirdly the thing is a bit soft, she wonders where it's gone, but she's already in flight, on her supersonic, roaring aeroplane, and off she goes.

When she puts her underpants back on, she sees a tiny spot of blood. Hardly worth making a fuss about.

She falls asleep watching the end of *Raiders of the Lost Ark*. Bihotz has disappeared then Bihotz comes back. The sky is clear in the east. He shouts about how idiotic it is that he's been kicked out of his own home when, fuck it, he lives here. She says, no way, she's never kicked him out, just like she doesn't paint her nails (she shows him), is he pretending she's someone else or what? The TV makes a *chrrrrrr* sound and the picture goes fuzzy. At her age she needs to sleep so why doesn't he just go out for a walk—walk as much as he wants. After that there's a strange lurching of the room as it folds in on them, the walls squash against each other and push them together, the ceiling has swapped places with the floor, and they have rolled, one on top of the other, one inside the other.

It's actually right inside her body (she can feel it), it must reach up to about where her bellybutton is, she'll have to measure it, she can't feel it all the way along but more or less at different spots. She manages to get him to plead with her about where she wants it ('tell me what you want'—if he'd just shut up with it now), it's not always easy to make him understand her, so she sits on top of him, it's so much more convenient, she goes at the rhythm she wants, she stretches back bit by bit like a bow (or like that alarm clock she used to wind up until it started ratcheting back on itself in a racket of tiny frenzied bells). Every single part of the tubular, layered, round, hollow and bulging area (like Barbapapa's house) of her cunt has been touched, rubbed, filled and emptied, pressed and squeezed—and it's really good, even better than when she masturbates, it's totally great.

Vulva n. ['vəlvə] The external genital organs of the woman and of the female in advanced animal species. ENCYCL. The vulva is formed on either side by the labia majora and the labia minor, and in the centre, front and back by the clitoris, urethra and the opening of the vagina, the latter partially sealed by the hymen in the case of virgins.

Vagina n. [və'jīnə] (lat. *vagina*, sheath). The passage leading from the opening of the vulva to the cervix of the uterus. ENCYCL. The vagina is the female organ of copulation; it is situated between the urethral opening and the anus.

Copulation n. (lat. *copulatio*, union). Coitus or sexual intercourse between a male and a female.

And a few days and nights and sunrises and late-night TV programmes later, they are still at it, having a go, trying to understand, doing it again so they can understand better, and so that—according to Bihotz—they can be done with it. Doing it again one last time, getting to the end of it, finishing up for good. As soon as they've put an end to it, it starts up again, they come together to be done with it, they struggle, entwined together, but the thing draws even more strength from their struggle. When they chop off one head, two more shoot forth; when they try to excise some of its flesh it redoubles its growth. Sometimes he yells that it's all his fault, or all her fault, that he only wanted to help out—what can they do, how can they get out of this thing. They start up again. She shows him how to press right here and slip his finger in there and lick her with his tongue right there, his dick grows big and fat again, so what can they do? Sometimes it's him on top and she rubs herself against his belly, sometimes it's him underneath and she rubs herself against him and it's even better.

They stop to eat and she goes to school and they sleep a bit and they take the dog outside and they play cards. Sometimes it doesn't work so they start up again, sometimes it's pretty ordinary so they start up again, sometimes they've had enough so they start up again, sometimes it's *so* great they start up again, she's really got to stop using 'so' all the time. In between their *ding-dongs* (they have invented their own vocabulary) the rest of the time is almost business as usual.

Rose has worked out a system, in a homework notebook, for filing her reading. Seven categories of books, from worst to best, arranged according to the days of the week. Monday, lousy. Tuesday, poor. Wednesday, average. Thursday, good. Friday, very good. Saturday, excellent. And Sunday, fantastic.

Her head is spinning. It's as if Rose is talking about her, her and Bihotz, about their week, but no, that's impossible.

Rose's characteristic enthusiasm means that she has catalogued most of the books under Friday and Saturday, very good and excellent. She's also created subdivisions, 'very good+' and 'excellent+'. She has been filing her reading since she was eleven, since she read *The Diary of Anne Frank*, which she liked so much that she invented the category 'super+' and decided that no other book could ever be better than that one.

That's a bit like sanitary napkins.

'You have a sick mind. Anyway, Anne Frank is the first writer ever in the world to have written about periods. There's nothing dirty about it at all.'

It's getting harder and harder to talk to Rose.

I thought she wrote about the concentration camps.

Rose's mouth opens wide, then she condescends to explain to her childhood friend, to her ignoramus childhood friend: 'She didn't write about the concentration camps, *precisely* because her diary stops when she's deported.' Rose is the keeper of knowledge that is so much more important than periods and fucking; it's knowledge that separates adults from non-adults, *historical* and *political* knowledge.

Politics is a sort of vast tilting globe of the world from which individual heads emerge, masses of them, appearing and disappearing. The grid lines are creased here and there around particular names and places. Clèves isn't marked at all. The past, made up of mountain ranges, takes up a lot of space, it's full of Egyptians and Chinese, and the future is a wide esplanade occupied by people who all have a cause. Rose's father, who reads *Le Monde Diplomatique*, moves his finger over the surface of the globe, tracing big circles that solve problems. The circles make huge fiery oil slicks around a microscopic central point: around her, Solange (peripheral and anxious, not central), Solange the *individual* (Solange is such a free spirit).

She can't help noticing Bihotz kneeling under his canna

lilies, weeding madly, his trowel and spray beside him.

Doesn't everyone have a cause?

'And what would be your cause?' Rose asks, annoyed.

Solange the free spirit, the individual, inside a snowball, her arms raised, calling for help. *I'm against racism. And against the atomic bomb* (she declares in order to gain time). *And against the killing of animals. Against the* systematic *killing of animals* (she adds) (one of her father's adjectives).

Rose's interest is sparked by *systematic*. 'And what do you actually do, to resist it?'

I think about it, she replies, with enough conviction to stand up to Rose's sniggering.

When her father was a pilot, she used to keep the planes in the air through the sheer power of her own thoughts, for as long as she could follow their flight path in the sky.

And she also gives butter to the birds in winter. Her mother has donated to the Ethiopians. *Of course* that's not the same thing, but alleviating suffering at home (and not simply tracing big circles with a compass), that's the way to change the world.

'Charity begins at home,' Rose says ironically. She's always got the knack of plucking the perfect sentence out of nowhere.

If she only knew, if Rose could just *glimpse* the week that she has had, it would take her down a peg or two. With an adult man. Who is almost *twice* her age. (Obviously she mustn't say who.)

She flips through the homework notebook. The category 'fantastic' is full of Boris Vian titles and so stuffed with 'so's that it's like Rose has run out of steam, through a lack of words, or what? (Does enthusiasm have anything to do with *orgasms*?) (Does Rose have *orgasms*?) At the other end, filed under 'lousy', there is only one book, Albert Cohen's *Belle du Seigneur* ('recommended by my mother').

His vision of women is so appalling, ridiculous, ludicrous. He wants her to love him while he wears the mask of a repulsive old man, whereas he would obviously not love her if she was horribly ugly or even just a little bit ugly. Does he even ask himself that question? Can you love a woman for her ~~inne beauty~~ her intelligence? Like when she has separate toilets built so that their love will last, as if their love had no real bodily functions. And the worst thing of all is the lack of punctuation when you're in her head, as if she had no idea about putting full stops at the end of sentences, it's such a phony sense of style. And the height of ludicrousness is when she calls having an orgasm taking her pleasure.

She stops there. (Orgasm?)

'It's the most ludicrous book I've ever read, but you might learn a few things,' Rose suggests.

How should she respond? If she argues with her then here comes trouble. *It's not just about learning, but about things going wrong. And it's not just about having a cosy little clean conscience. I've been through some traumatic stuff.*

Rose doesn't get it. Or at least she doesn't get the connection.

You remember when my father flashed his dick at the carnival?

Rose still doesn't get it.

When he pulled out his thing? In front of everyone?

'Your father has never been a flasher. He was just a loser.'

She's speaking about him as if he was dead. (A flasher?) (A loser?) It's always the same whenever she goes to Rose's: the planet shifts on its axis, there's ice at the equator and a thaw at both poles, everything's upside down up, unrecognisable—the oceans and the land, her father and her mother, and Clèves.

I saw him, right in front of me, in front of the priest, it was midnight, he was with his mate Georges from the yacht club, and everyone saw him and I was convinced that that was it, that I could never face anyone ever again.

'I do remember one carnival when your father and Georges were completely pissed, that's right. We'd gone on the dodgem cars with Christian (oh my God, we were so young!). But the rest of your story is complete bullshit, you must have been smoking too much dope. Firstly, it wasn't midnight (we weren't allowed out that late). Secondly, he never showed his dick, I would have remembered that.'

(The dodgem cars blinking under the electric sky. And Christian with his baby face.)

'My mother says that your father is always trying to make out that he's got a big dick. But that's just an expression. It's not *literal*,' Rose continues (incomprehensible, as usual). She rummages in her bag (a real leather handbag, for women) and takes out a tampon, show-off, like it's a gutsy thing to do, as if she's the first girl in the world to be on the rag. She leaves the room without a word. There's a fragrance in the air—soap, roses and cleaning products.

As for her, she hasn't used a tampon yet. It must be a while since it's been that time of the month for her. Her cunt is driving her crazy, it's so itchy, sticky and swollen like an overripe pear. Too much fucking.

Bihotz takes her out for dinner. He's chosen a restaurant miles away. Of course everyone has seen them together in Clèves, but they weren't *together* like they are today. She's never thought of it like that before.

Attack of the itchy cunt again. By tipping her pubic bone forward and sliding her buttocks so her underpants are dragged to the side, she makes contact with the cold fake leather of the car seat and gets some relief. She likes the smell of this van. Of this Peugeot J7. Before, it used to smell of hay, petrol, rabbit. Now there's a smell that makes something leap inside her chest (not her heart, that would be *laughable*).

Clèves recedes in the rear-vision mirror, the J7 gains speed and she wants never to return to the village, to its mushroom houses and its child-eating children, she'd like to unwind from its ribbon road (and they all lived happily ever after and had, no, didn't have any children).

She puts her hand on Bihotz's shoulder and he turns to her (he's got the eyes of a gentle troll who has just captured the princess). What they need is for the night to swallow them up, for the night to become a cave where he can keep her concealed. Life in a cave with Bihotz.

Take her pleasure, what's wrong with saying take her pleasure?

'In two or three years,' murmurs Bihotz as he gently peels her hands off him, 'in two or three years we'll be able to go out together properly.'

She had clung to him, stupidly shy. She hadn't been expecting this kind of restaurant. Smart waiters and fancy white tablecloths. She'd imagined the sea, a toasted cheese sandwich with Australian surfers, bars filled with Kim Wilde's voice. Under the lampshades, Bihotz is glowing, smiling. He's tied back his hair, he looks different.

'You are very pretty.'

She nicked Lætitia's eyeliner and worked out the right technique: smear it on the eyelid and then rub off the extra bit with a cotton bud. (Obviously no one must come into the bathroom during the procedure.)

'The appetizer,' announces the waiter.

They dive into tiny bowls of orange mousse with lumpfish roe. She sticks up her little finger like rich people do; she's wearing the butterfly rings her father gave her the day of her twelfth birthday. It's so cool to eat without having to set the table. Bihotz orders the fish soup and the kidneys in Madeira sauce with *gratin dauphinois* (and he hesitates over the *confit de canard*). The waiter has seated them near the fireplace.

You could burn a whole tree in there. Just like in castles in the Middle Ages.

The *confit* would have been a better choice after all. *The* gratin dauphinois *is to die for.* She'd like to ask for seconds but they're not at the school canteen.

'I'm not going to go overboard with the lentils,' says Bihotz as he places his knife and fork across his plate. 'They cause flatulence.'

She remembers Madame Bihotz saying, 'It's tasty but it's a taste that leaves you wanting more.'

'When you leave your cutlery like this,' he explains to her, 'it means that you've had enough.'

Everything's shining. The waiters in black and white move back and forth, with little entrechat leaps as they twirl between the tables, performing some sort of acrobatics with their plates and their incredible sentences.

Suddenly all the lights go out and in the dark a blaze of yellow comes towards them—a cake for a neighbouring table crowded with uncles and grandmothers, a strawberry gateau specially ordered for the eleventh birthday of a virginal young girl who looks like she'd wear panty liners.

Can't I have a dessert?

He looks at her as if she's said something that was at the same time idiotic and inspired, as if she was a young queen who should be showered with chocolate, tiaras and kisses, glass slippers (which must really hurt your feet) and silver carriages. Something's bothering him but he can't find it in himself to ask her.

Yes, you can. Ask me.

She orders the chocolate fondant with crème anglaise and she'd like another glass of the 1978 Haut-Médoc.

'How many boys have you already had relationships with?'

You'd think it was a lady with a perm asking her how many lollipops she'd like. The pretty English boy (what was his name again?), and the fireman? That'd make two. Three with him, Bihotz (but is she *going out* with Bihotz?). (If she's *going out* with anyone it's Arnaud—four.)

I don't know, around ten? She licks the heavy solid-silver spoon. *First there was a surfer, and before that there was Christian but we didn't fuck, and now there's Raphaël Bidegarraï who wants to go out with me. But right now I've got Arnaud, you know that. That makes* (she counts on her fingers) *three months and two weeks and four days—my record.*

She's crucifying him. Why is she doing it? Doesn't he want to stop her, can't he stand up for himself and show who the real man is, right now?

He lights a cigarette and blows the smoke up towards

the ceiling. 'How long will it be before you use the familiar form and say *tu* to me?'

The fire is glowing, red and gold, in the bottom of her glass of Haut-Médoc. It's raining now, pattering on the roof of the restaurant, the flames are dancing, and out the window nature is seething in a feverish sunset.

She focuses on the last spoonfuls of crème anglaise.

It's funny, I've already eaten the chocolate fondant and it's already in my stomach and I still have the taste on my tongue and soon we're going to leave the table and what I'm saying to you, right now, is like the fine line, the very extreme limit between past and future. And, can't you see, that's what we call the present? That's all it is! What we're experiencing right now is already the past and we're straight into the future. What we're experiencing now literally *doesn't exist, can't you see? It's already finished, it's already slipped between our fingers, like the crème anglaise, it's nothing at all, how do I get to think this stuff?*

A big lump of emotion threatens to gag her (is she going to vomit?).

'My mother didn't let me drink at your age.'

He's whispering but it's like he's screaming. The last thing she needs is for him to be his mother. He pays. He leaves a few five-franc coins, just like that, for show. She breathes deeply, leaning on his arm, scrutinised by the menagerie of waiters—no more playing cat and mouse for those sly foxes.

The countryside has melted in the rain. The horizon is quivering in the distance, the beaded light glancing back at them. Everything is misty, pretty, imitation Japanese. A soggy owl makes its *whoo ooh* and flaps its wings.

Primary school rhymes come back to her, about the rain in Spain and the honey and money, of the owl, the elegant fowl, and the pussycat, hand in hand, on the edge of the sand, eating with a runcible spoon, dancing by the light of the moon.

In the sweet-smelling J7, Bihotz goes for her, too hard, too fast, trying to grab her, hold her, so that instead of (it doesn't take much) thinking only about skewering herself on it (jamming it in, ramming it in, mounting it, milking it, moaning for it) she gives him a bit of a hand job (a bursting sausage in her butterfly-ringed fingers) and then she stops, we're not animals.

'Oh, come on,' begs Bihotz.

She holds back for a bit when he chews the inside of her thighs, but it feels so good, and when he puts his tongue in and then rubs his palm there like she's shown him how to, it's absolutely unbearable—she pushes him back and sits on top of him, a *ding-dong* between the steering wheel and the gear stick, he comes very fast but so does she, that's lucky. Her itchy cunt is calm again.

She can't help reciting a poem from her childhood, by Maurice Carême. She must be completely drunk. He opens the window and lights a Marlboro. In the darkness (not a single light, not a single house) he's almost good-looking. Colossal, manly. It would be so practical to be in love with him. It would solve the whole issue of the future, what to do, what to think, all the problems. They'd live together, her parents next door. They'd have a baby boy that she'd give to her parents. (She must get her head around the whole pill thing, etc.) They would pretend to be together for real, while floods and catastrophes engulfed the world.

That reminds me of one of my father's jokes (she laughs so loudly that she has to stop and rest for a moment). *A travelling salesman books into a hotel, he's exhausted and all that, but there's a knock on the door of his room and a really young girl says to him* (Solange imitates the voice of the really young girl): *'For ten francs I'll do it to you with one hand, for twenty francs I'll do it with two hands, and for thirty francs I'll do it with my tongue as well!' So even though he's exhausted and all that, he says fine, fine, he gives her thirty francs and the young girl goes: nananabooboo!* She sticks out her tongue and wiggles her hands like rabbit ears.

He looks at her in silence.

He's so hard to talk to, he's just *so* boring when it comes to conversation.

Orgasm ['ôr,gazəm] n. (from Greek *organ*, to mature, to swell). The most intense point during sexual excitement, sexual intercourse, sexual congress.

Sexual congress ['sek SH ōōəl 'kä NG grəs] n. The act of sexual procreation between a man and a woman. Having to do with sexual reproduction.

Reproduction [ˌrēprə'də sʜ ən] n. Any of various processes by which an animal or plant produces one or more individuals similar to itself. | | An imitation or facsimile of a work of art. | | The quality of sound from an audio system. | | The act or process of reproducing. | | A revival of an earlier production, as of a theatrical play.

'Most women don't like it,' Nathalie pronounces.

There's that song by Brassens, 'Ninety-five times out of a hundred, the woman gets bored during sex.' And all those articles about frigidity and the *postpartum period* and lighting incense and putting on soft music and starting with a massage.

Real women are *vaginistic*, according to Nathalie. The others are *clitoristic*. The main thing is to find the G-spot.

'Men are looking for the Holy Grail, women are looking for the G,' says Rose sarcastically. (Nobody reacts because nobody understands.)

Concepción said she wouldn't come over anymore because we only spoke about horrible things, but in the end she turned up. Delphine came too (she still has purple hair but apparently she's got over her *tragic gesture*). Her mother tolerates their little get-togethers at Rose's—even though the parents are left-wing, they're good people. But no one sees Lætitia anymore since it's got around that she's a dyke.

What a fuss.

'She's just a snob,' says Rose. 'Anyway, what would she see in you?'

Rose's room is impeccably organised (they have a cleaning lady) and she hasn't got anything stuck on her walls, everything's so white, so trendy. They're allowed to smoke here (only tobacco). The ashtray is an enormous lump of glass with bubbles inside. They drink tea from a very heavy teapot. Rose is lounging in a black wood and leather armchair she has nicked from her parents.

What a performance.

'When I was on language exchange in England,' she begins, 'there was this Lebanese guy who'd been living in the residential college since the beginning of the Lebanese Civil War. He was'—she lights a cigarette—'much older than me, he had a room to himself, well not exactly but his roommate had gone away and he offered me a massage. He put a chair against the door to stop anyone coming in, and he massaged my back. He went down past my waist, massaged my buttocks and it was only when he started to massage between my thighs that I started to wonder…'

Concé is getting stressed. Everyone bursts out laughing.

'He massaged me right where you're imagining and I could feel him rubbing his dick against my buttocks. And I said to myself, what was I thinking? Nothing's for free in this capitalist society. So we made love.'

She laughs. So everyone laughs.

This story doesn't fit at all with the image of the blood-bath—of the *butchering* that Nathalie told her about after Rose had told Nathalie about her deflowering in this same residential college (so she did it again?).

'And your surfer?' Nathalie asks her, Solange. It's a trick.

She heaves a little sigh of rapture. She can't talk about it (her surfer), it was too great, too amazing, they wouldn't understand.

She told Nathalie everything about Bihotz, begging her not to say anything to anyone, or only to talk about it using the word 'surfer'. Nathalie understands the *sex project*: how she's sleeping with Bihotz because Arnaud isn't around. She just changed a few details (*with Arnaud I discovered what real sexual pleasure is*) ('it's true that you don't orgasm in the same way when the relationship is serious'—*it creates a real bond*—'to orgasm like that is real love, that's for sure'). They did the *Marie-Claire* quiz about the difference between *loving* and *being in love*: from an emotional point of view, there's no comparison. And what is certain is that you can't love two guys at the same time.

There are girls who think a lot, like Rose or Lætitia, and girls who live hard, who feel things intensely, and that (as Nathalie said) is incalculable, you can't put a price on it, that's what life is really about, in the end the body speaks the truth—Rose doesn't get it.

*

Bihotz has bought her an inflatable pool, the biggest he could find, she can do two breaststrokes across it (she bangs into the other side). He pours in two tubs of hot water so that she can get in without freezing.

Maman has gone away to have a rest somewhere.

The population of Clèves has reached a new milestone—2500 inhabitants—the difference between a village and a town. From now on we live in a town. The central business district of Clèves now even boasts a bakery and a driving school.

Rose has come over to try out the new tennis game that Bihotz has loaded on the TV. There are two *joysticks* connected to a box with wires, a vertical line in the middle of the screen and two little white lines that bat a square of white light back and forth. It's fun.

He's weeding again, wearing his wolf T-shirt, which has had its fair share of outings, and which he only wears now for 'outside' jobs.

'You've always been a bit rustic,' laughs Rose. 'You've got to go out with someone in the same league as you.'

Rose knows. About Bihotz. Even though she's under the influence of Bidegarraï, she's teasing her in a kind way. With (even?) a hint of admiration in her voice. Bihotz. An adult, working-class, and even a bit of a *misfit*. 'Regarded as a misfit,' Rose adds.

(And her father, regarded as a loser?)

She can see herself in a few years' time, lying by a

brick swimming pool, drinking red and yellow cocktails with straws and little umbrellas (there are heaps of them at the Kudeshayans). There she'd be, in Clèves, in the sun, Bihotz would be looking after her in his misfit way, she'd play sport, she would have lost five kilos, she'd watch TV and get into reading, crosswords and nouvelle-cuisine cooking.

'Love is stronger than the class struggle,' Rose says approvingly.

She can glimpse a future full of romance and confrontation. Everyone in the village confused. Her divorced parents opposing the union. She and Bihotz escaping on the first available plane with the help, finally, of her father. She and her father embracing on the tarmac. In his parting adieu, he says he loves her.

She cries a little as she jiggles her feet in the pool. She'd like to live by the sea but it's too expensive, and even if Bihotz sold his mother's dump of a house, what would they get for it, a little studio without even a view and then what would they do?

Nathalie says that the whole thing with Bihotz is ridiculous.

In a little studio with Arnaud. By a pool with Arnaud. Panting and arched over.

'Let's go away,' says Bihotz. 'Let's fill the J7 with canned food and leave. What's stopping us? I'll find work doing odd jobs. We'll renovate run-down houses. We'll plant vegetable gardens. We'll reinvent life, you'll see. We don't have to do anything we don't want to. We'll find some place right by the sea and we'll stare at it for as long as you like.'

He's started tinkering again. He's taken out the back seats of the J7 in preparation for an elaborate wooden construction that he's drawn to plan and cut out with the jigsaw, including rounded corners and recesses. He's making them a bed, with pull-down bedside tables and little bedside lights—during the day they'll be able to fold up the bed and use it as a bench. He's aiming for a cushioned but uncluttered effect, all in curves and jointed panels, like the interior of the spaceship in *2001* (they just watched the movie again together on TV).

Everything's in the joinery, he announces. It's got to be smooth, so that you can't feel any imperfections and you can't detect any of the joins when you look at it. It's in the gaps, in what is uneven, unglued, badly squared off, that things collect—like dirt and chaos, disunion, discord, evil.

It's raining on the little swimming pool but it's nice in the house.

Lulu is taking forever to die; when she's dead we'll be able to leave, there'll be nothing more to keep us here. He spreads out road maps and traces the routes with his finger, curving roads highlighted in green, all spreading out from Clèves, which has turned into a minuscule town in a shrunken corner of a microscopic country.

Take a plane and cross the ocean, with Arnaud. New York. Los Angeles. Hawaii.

Bihotz comes in from the garden and tells her that the weather is improving.

Arnaud coming home from work. He's an engineer. A computer specialist. Guitarist. He tells her about his day, the people, the world.

She practises concentrating, so she can try to grasp the difference between the two of them, the different lives and different futures.

An apartment in town. Arnaud has other women. She has to fight to keep him. To stick to her promises. A guy like him would motivate her to get ahead.

Bihotz asks her if she's finished her homework. She is stuck in limbo. Like those characters in *Star Trek* when the transporter breaks down and they're dematerialised in space-time.

Sure, there'll be more of them (boys) (that's what Rose and Nathalie keep banging on about) (it's not like you're going to get pregnant and be, like, forced to marry him) (Nathalie screeches in horror).

But what if there weren't any more? It's already undreamed of that she has *a choice.* It would be better to know what the future will be, and then wait for it without doing anything anymore, like Lulu. A life of being pampered versus a life of adventure.

She has a vision of herself by the pool (the big, brick one) sipping a fruit cocktail while Bihotz is weeding, or by the phone, waiting for Arnaud—he's coming home, he's coming back. He puts his helmet down (he has a motorbike). He undoes the fly on his biker pants and nods at her. She runs over, panting, she takes out his dick and licks it, he remains impassive, grabs her hair and makes her gradually swallow up his inordinately large dick, deep into the back of her throat. He takes his time and she gets *wet like a bitch.*

She stares up at the ceiling, a faraway look in her eyes and a faraway feeling in her body. Bihotz's voice interrupts her—'Lunch is served.' For a while now he's been making jokes that are not funny. And his face is changing. He never stops smiling, as if he was a bit frightened. And when they've finished their *ding-dong*, he often says to her, half-laughing, 'It wasn't me who taught you how to do all that.'

She puts her hand out to him (they'd had a fight earlier—he was missing a hundred francs and supposedly she'd taken them). She pulls down her underpants and sticks his face between her legs. When she's had enough, she can see that he looks different again: glistening, slimy, like a fish; that shrouded gaze, its impenetrable force, which sees nothing but wants everything, and wants an end to it—the emptiness of that gaze that has no name.

Bihotz.

He snaps out of it and looks at her now with a tenderness that is worse than the other look. A good old loving gaze from the old days, an incredibly sweet gaze for my angel, Solange.

She rolls over onto her belly, at least she doesn't have

to look at him anymore. He pats her hair but she shakes her head—she pushes her hips in the air, inviting him. He throws himself into it immediately, enthusiastically, but that's not where she wants it, she guides him higher up. 'Are you sure?' and 'I'm not hurting you?' and lots of 'Oh my darling'.

She starts squealing like the girls on Canal Plus, so he'll shut up. And that gives her a funny feeling, to be both directing the film and acting in it. She pushes her fingers down to rub herself, she lets Arnaud enter her, his biker pants, she focuses on the script—Angie, you've really got a lot of potential, bitch bitch bitch, soon she'll start yapping. It feels rough and hard, horribly abrasive, she's going to die if she doesn't come. She's got several minds, several bodies—one in the film, one on the couch, both looking at each other, one putting witty words into Arnaud's mouth, the other directing the right rhythm for Bihotz's hips—and a non-stop tick tock of an alarm clock running backwards, counting down this time of hers that is so exasperating, restricted, and fit to burst—

'You are a strange girl, Solange,' he says when they get their breath again (in his accent that makes 'ange' rhyme with 'mange').

He's got a bit of poo on the end of his dick.

'I'm so touched, Solange. It's such a token of your confidence that you have given me right now...'

She's going to kill him if he doesn't shut up.

The next day, he leaves very early for the market in

the clucking J7, to sell all his chickens. When he gets back they have a huge fight because he wants to give Lulu an injection, he says it's the only solution, she yells at him that she'll report him to the cops if he does.

'Solange, I have to talk to you,' says Rose's mother when they're having afternoon tea at Rose's house.

She's always had trouble finding her way around Rose's house. It's an old farmhouse that they've gutted, in which (like inside a whale) you wander around along ramps, mezzanines, staircases—she's only just realised this instant that the father's study is right next to the kitchen, whereas she would have gone the long way round, room after room, unwinding the house like a ball of twine.

'Is it true, what Rose has told me? Has someone hurt you, Solange?' What have Rose (and Nathalie) told her?

Rose's mother is very intimidating. But there's something in her red boots—this woman gets away with red boots when no one else wears them—something that suggests she might perhaps understand. Don't we have the right to do what we want? (What do you want, Solange?)

'Is everything all right, Solange?'

It's Arnaud. But he lives in Bordeaux now, so everything's not all right.

'Do you want to come and live at our place in the meantime?'

At their place? At Rose's house? But does Rose's father know about it? There he is in his study, devoted to his Committee for the Defence of the Rights of the Indigenous Peoples of Chiapas. In this house that is full of such beautiful objects. And there are Rose's parents, who always do everything perfectly, who understand everything about everything. Her brain is completely scrambled—as soon as she has one idea another one comes and skittles it and it just keeps going like that, knocking over every square on the board, one by one; instead of making quick connections, she has to follow the whole path around the board and her brain gets stuck—as if it's between two mirrors, reflected all the way to the vanishing point, she and Bihotz, she and Arnaud.

'Seriously, Solange, are you using contraception?'

Peggy Salami changed foster families quite a few times. She left Clèves recently and was placed in a hostel, (apparently) so that she wouldn't get pregnant (people like that should be sterilised, Georges said). Are they going to leave her with the Department of Human Services?

It's so itchy down there. Rose's mother doesn't seem to understand.

She can feel the corners of her mouth forming creases, the creases that mean she's going to cry, her chin wobbles and a huge bucket of tears spills, they pour down her like seeds, she points between her thighs. It really is itchy. Perhaps it's (she's terrified now) the first symptoms of the disease, the disease where you die in two years?

'Vaginal fungal infections are common in the beginning, it's nothing to worry about, just fungi, hasn't your mother taken you to see someone?'

Rose's mother opens a little notebook with a silver clasp. She talks on the phone while mushroom propagation is taking place in the humus of Solange's cunt: cep mushrooms, chanterelles, trumpet of death mushrooms and puffballs. Everything in this house is clean and tidy and scrubbed—it's another world, a world where these things down inside her, these *misfit* things, do not grow.

Arnaud is singing over the top of the radio: 'Like a virgin, oh oh oh,' he's hamming it up, he's so funny. 'That Madonna chick has really got it. She overdoes the virgin so she can play up the whore. She'll have an amazing career. If you can't see the difference between her and Kim Wilde, you're just not with it.'

He's forgotten to put in his contact lenses and he's driving with his nose against the windscreen. She'd like to stroke his back (but she doesn't dare). There's a copy of *Le Monde* scattered under the seats. She doesn't know any other boy who reads *Le Monde.* This is Clèves, fishing competitions, new roundabouts, diamond wedding anniversaries and cattle shows.

Kim Wilde is sweet, she's nicer. And I think she's much more attractive.

'Who gives a stuff about attractive? It's her tits that matter.'

He's making fun of the local louts. A bit like Madonna does with women. That's the problem when everything he says is tongue-in-cheek: you never know exactly what he's saying.

Kim Wilde shows her bra.

'I'm sceptical. Kim Wilde is your typical good girl. A bit wimpy, not wild, the sort of girl who gets all reproachful after you've done it, and if you marry her she'll think she's won the lottery. Madonna will end up leaving you, but she'll be fun while you're having her.'

The car is heading towards a world without Kim Wilde. There's still time to go back to the cave with Bihotz (Bihotz loves Kim Wilde almost as much as France Gall, and he would know what she's trying to say, that the most important thing is *kindness*).

Arnaud lets go of the gearstick for a second to take her hand and plants a kiss on it, she could die of happiness. Then he puts it on his fly, she rummages inside boxer shorts full of pubic hair and pulls out the dick, she jerks him off the way he likes it, not too hard, not too tight.

He parks behind the new apartment block they've built on the site of the old gravel pit. In the village, the d'Urbide chateau used to be the only building over two storeys. This is not the moment to be wondering about the passage of time, right now he's urging her to suck him off as well, 'If you love me, you have to swallow.' Whether or not that's tongue-in-cheek, he holds her head firmly so she doesn't miss a drop. Afterwards he's kind enough to offer her a piece of chewing gum. So that when the door opens and Jennifer greets Arnaud with a peck on the lips, she is chewing a gob of about fifty million spermatozoa, the population of France, strawberry-flavoured and swirling around in her mouth.

She'd like a glass of water. She throws the chewing gum in the bin in the kitchenette. Then she retrieves it and sticks it inside a napkin ring monogrammed *Jeannine*.

'I'm sceptical,' says Arnaud. It's his new word. He's commenting on the wallpaper that was hung on the weekend by the fabulous Jennifer's parents. It's yellow. The curtains match, there's a black sofa bed, yellow and black pouffes, a low wicker table, and a hyperrealist poster of an enormous dripping tube of yellow paint. It looks like a painting on top of paint. It makes you a bit dizzy. As if the picture was a representation of itself. Or like when you see a truck transporting a truck. Or like when you think about thinking. It also vaguely conjures up sex. She'd have trouble explaining why.

She's hungry but there's nothing in the fridge. Not even a crust of bread. She's never seen a kitchen like it. From where she's standing, she can see Arnaud and this so-called Jennifer, sitting side by side sharing a beer. They look a bit like Solange's parents did when they were young, in their black-and-white wedding photo. From the louvre window she can see Arnaud's car (actually it's his mother's car). She feels like Kiki the soft toy monkey, nothing about any of this is really true.

They're supposed to be waiting for a guy called Fred and a guy called Jean-Marc who have apparently gone to find some dope, and also someone called Stéphane, who's in charge of booze. Véro should be arriving on her motorbike but it's not definite. Arnaud opens some more beers. 'Come and sit with us, Angie.'

'Is that her real name?' Jennifer asks.

Much later, another Jean-Marc (not the one they were expecting) comes by to tell them that there's a party at Franck's but that he doesn't have a car, and a guy with a girl studying nursing has set himself up in front of the cassette recorder to listen to the latest Police single, and Arnaud and Jennifer haven't stopped kissing on the sofa bed. But she's got to be broad-minded, Jennifer is in Year 12 and she's Arnaud's official girlfriend (in addition to the one from Bordeaux). She, Solange, is the secret favourite (not to mention how young she is). The only one who knows—she's the one he tells everything to.

That's what he explains to her in the kitchenette when she demands that he take her home. She was allowed out to midnight (and only because she told Bihotz that she was going to see *Flashdance* with Nathalie). Arnaud tells her that she's pissing him off with her whole Cinderella line. To which she replies that in fact she has to go home to *be with her boyfriend*. With whom *she lives*.

One thing leads to another and they're in the car park behind the building and Arnaud is saying again that he is sceptical, really sceptical. That he doesn't know who to trust anymore. Or what he should believe about how things seem. That it's not going to be possible. He doesn't share. How can a girl like you be shared? Who is the other guy?

She describes the surfer with the peeling lips and Arnaud pins her against the car, and while she outlines the plans for their trip and how they're fitting out their van, he has already pulled down her underpants and the car door is very hard against her buttocks—she can't feel much else but it's terribly exciting, metal on skin, glass and flesh, hot and cold—and the thrilling possibility that Jennifer is looking out the louvre window of the kitchenette! Or that someone will suddenly turn up in the car park!

He starts again a bit further away (in the Clèves forest). Arnaud says that he wants her all to himself, that it's driving him crazy. She lies back and moans: she is beautiful, desirable, a woman, a woman with you, I finally felt like a woooman, like in that Nicole Croisille song her mother loves, she arches back a bit more and her hair catches on the windscreen wipers, help, he's ramming it into her even harder, it hurts a bit and her coccyx is going *clunk-clunk* on the icy bonnet, but as long as he looks at her, and doesn't make a mess of it, as long as he screws her, gives it to her, works her over properly. As hard as she tries to picture herself in her mind—to picture the whole set-up, expanding the number of images and imagining herself as both Arnaud and this woman *offering herself*—she gets nowhere. Too bad, anyway he's finished.

'Where will we go?' Arnaud asks.

She's recaptured that marvellous connection with him. Where they can talk *so* well together about things... The future will take shape at last, they'll be together again: after all these twists and turns they will finally be able to live together in love, he'll be all hers, and she'll be all his.

Why don't we go to the sea?

He thinks that's a great idea. He's seeing the real Solange now. That's it, now he really understands her: romantic and whimsical, funnier than he'd expected, and more seductive too. He must love her, for sure. Otherwise he wouldn't be driving this far.

The road heads out among the lighthouses. Villages, fields, villages. They're singing along to a Michel Jonasz song, *Even one day spent without her, It's sorrow, And my heart on the end of a string, Hanging*, he's holding the steering wheel with one hand and sticking his other hand in her pussy. It hurts a bit (his guitarist's nails) but it's funny too, she's never seen anyone driving in this position before. *And the storms passed and we were... the creeks and the cliffs, Ice and a furnace, Heat from the embers.* This is real life, a man, a car and singing. In the moonlight the sea stretches the windscreen to the size of her happiness—she's made it, this is exactly what she wanted, her heart filled with dreams of the sea, sensuality, and a future of tough times followed by peace.

The sand dune is all sand (not even a tiny bit of grass so she can avoid getting itchy). She lies languidly on his shoulder listening to him breathe over the murmur of the waves. The Whole Universe. What her mother talks about, but for real. They're part of the cosmos and the stars are twinkling, and if they set out straight across the water they would see the Statue of Liberty rising up into the sky. 'Montreal is straight ahead,' Arnaud corrects her. Montreal is fine too.

In the car she tries discreetly to get rid of the sand; it's set off her thrush again.

The sun is rising when he drops her outside Bihotz's house. There's a light on in the kitchen. She's in for it.

Bihotz's face is all puffy from crying. Lulu is on the formica table, wrapped up in Madame Bihotz's patchwork quilt, stiff as a board.

Damn.

She'll wait until tomorrow (well, whenever she wakes up) to tell him that they've got to stop. In the meantime, she's dying of hunger, because she and Arnaud didn't eat at all. She gets out some leftover chicken from the fridge ('wait, let me heat it up for you'), it's a bit awkward eating in front of him (and not that appetising with Lulu dead right there, but he's in the middle of wiping everything down with bleach).

Poor Monsieur Bihotz. She was especially kind so he'd have happy memories of her. It was a bit weird doing it so quickly after Arnaud. Perhaps the two sets of sperm cancel each other out? Like in a physics class, when you put water in a test-tube with oxygen and it explodes, leaving just a tiny bit of vapour?

It's touching when he snores, his nose still blocked from being so emotional before. He *so* deserves to be loved. And perhaps in another life, in other *circumstances*—but it's like his dick doesn't really make him into a man. In any case not a man like her father or like Arnaud. It's tiring to think about all that. She tries to get up, she doesn't want to sleep there—she's got to get up.

Dear Monsieur Bihotz,

I have left with Arnaud. I have chosen my path. I'm sorry but I'd rather tell you because I don't want to hurt you. I send you my sincere condolences for Lulu. I know it will annoy you that I'm saying this but you know soon you'll get another replacement dog. I wanted to thank you for all the good times we've had together. Forget me and start a new life. I'll never forget you. Lots of kisses.

Solange.

P.S. Don't make a fuss or else I'll tell everyone.

♥♥♥♥

Bihotz is in his garden, he looks like he's getting on just fine. He's banging and tapping on something.

Arnaud said he'd be coming. She doesn't know yet whether she's going to be living in Bordeaux with him, or if he's got somewhere else in mind (because of his *official* girlfriend).

Her heart leaps when she hears the garden gate open, but it's her mother, who is dropping by briefly to collect the mail and check that everything's okay.

'Are you eating properly?' Her mother has lost a lot of weight (or got old). She's found an internship for herself in a language camp at a farm, French immersion for students (except that because of the shop she's saddled with two hours of driving a day). Being married is one of the main reasons behind her *amputating* herself from her roots, what with the scorn Solange's father has for everything she is, all her values—for the way she lives her life like a tourist, as he calls it, and for what he claims is her colonialist vision, yes! As well as the scorn he has for the female experience.

Thank goodness she can relax knowing Monsieur Bihotz is here. He shouldn't worry. Papa must be sending him a cheque soon. She'll visit them again soon when she has more time. Give me a big kiss, my darling. Lots of kisses for my big girl. Everything will be better very soon.

She could even come and live at the language camp, on the farm.

Lulu is dead (she tells her mother on the doorstep).

'Poor Monsieur Bihotz. Be kind to him. I trust you.'

He's still banging away outside. Perhaps he's weeding—with more fervour than usual? From her bedroom window, she can see him under the oak trees. He's digging a hole. Breaking up the earth with huge swings of his spade. Acorns, last year's leaves, the spring catkin flowers. His big frame sends everything flying as he mulches it all up.

Did he find her letter? She put it under his pillow. And what if he tells everyone? What if she got sent to reform school? What if they took her away from Arnaud?

Their eyes meet, she quickly shuts the curtains with Statues of Liberty all over them.

Monsieur Bihotz is in hospital. He drank weedkiller. Rose's mother tells her, with a funny look on her face. Apparently he drank weedkiller *on purpose*. And if he doesn't die he'll probably lose his kidneys.

Kidneys are for peeing. And you can eat them.

Her brain is frozen, congealed in a white sauce. She has a vision of herself back at the restaurant with him, her plate of kidneys in front of her. She's always regretted not ordering the *confit de canard*. The girl at the next table, the birthday virgin, had ordered the *confit*. Perhaps everything might have been different if she had. Perhaps then Bihotz wouldn't have the kidney problem. But if Stalin, let's say, hadn't gone to Yalta, it wouldn't necessarily have changed the world, given that it would have been a *different* world.

'What could make an old bachelor like Bihotz behave like a schoolgirl? Don't tell me it was that old dog dying? People can be way too sentimental.'

Rose's father was very disturbed (so they say) by what Delphine did. Anyway it's nice to be able to walk around under his watchful eye without feeling judged or worried about getting a bad name (the worst thing would be for this man to think of her as being like Slurp or, worse still, like Delphine). According to Rose her mother is sexually frustrated. You wouldn't think it looking at Rose's father.

The other news item is that Nathalie is apparently a virgin. Christian wanted to try his luck with her (given how much she led him on by always talking about doing it) but she explained to him in the strictest confidence that she was saving herself for when she was ready, like for the love of her life.

Bullshit. She was just freaked out, that's all.

*

Her mother has come to pick her up from Rose's house. They're supposed to be visiting Monsieur Bihotz. She has as little desire to go and see Bihotz as she did to turn up at Delphine's bedside. Those sort of things just make her too sad.

'You're so selfish! Just like your father. Do you realise that Monsieur Bihotz is going to be on dialysis for the rest of his life?'

> (**Dialysis** [dī'aləsis] n. (from Greek *dialusis,* meaning dissolution). The separation of smaller molecules from larger molecules in a solution by selective diffusion through a semipermeable membrane. | | *Peritoneal dialysis,* a therapeutic method of eliminating metabolic waste from the body in cases of renal failure.)

It sounds a bit like a female first name. It turns out he's going to be attached to a machine. And he'll probably have to move house to be closer to the hospital, on the coast.

Arnaud is taking his time to turn up. He must have gone back to Bordeaux and most likely his girlfriend is making a scene.

And apparently her mother is angry with Rose's mother. Something about how offended she was that she had interfered by organising a gynaecologist for Solange (who cancelled the appointment anyway, given that she's with Arnaud). When the time comes, she says, she'll make the appointment herself for Solange. That woman and her red boots, she's really got some peculiar ideas about things.

As for her, she still hasn't got to try out tampons (it's an advantage not being a virgin). Rose's mother gave her a whole lecture about contraception—'no boy will ever worry about it on your behalf'—but Monsieur Bihotz did, after all, he's so responsible, he must have thought about it somehow or other. She remembers how he'd set out her first sanitary napkins next to his shaving cream. And how poetic he'd been comparing the shape of a bloodstain on the sheet to a 'moth'. She's almost moved by the thought of it.

Anyway, for someone young like her, it would be such a hassle—oh well, all that stuff is so boring. (She's got to stop using 'so' all the time.) She's got so many other things to think about.